A Marathon of Running

by

Stuart Macfarlane

Published by
Tattie Bogle Publishing

First Published October 2017

Copyright Stuart Macfarlane

ISBN: 9781521919132

Introduction

Runners! They are on our streets! They are in our parks! They bound in droves along our country trails! They are everywhere! Never in the history of mankind have so many people been prepared to leave the comfort of their homes and plod the cruel roads wearing little more than their underwear. Running has reached pandemic level and there seems to be no cure for this obsessive condition.

What is causing this? Is it because our television programs are now so terminally boring? Have our pubs started selling poor quality beer and wine? Has there been a universal plummeting of our sex drive that causes us to eject from our unconsummated beds at 7am each morning? Or has something in our DNA changed causing the widespread masochism that now makes the pain of running for miles somehow a feeling to be cherished?

Whatever the cause, the problem has now reached crisis level. You are now more likely to win a prize on the National Lottery than be successful in the ballot for the London Marathon. Even races of fifty gruelling mountainous miles have been known to sell out within minutes of online entry opening.

If you are one of the afflicted, you will enjoy this book, for you are sure to identify with the obsession that often makes what we do so very, very amusing. If you are one of the few people who do not take to the streets five times a week to torture your body you are guaranteed a few laughs at the expense of those of us who do. So, take some time off from your training (or from your burgers and beer if you are a non-runner), sit back, relax and enjoy.

[Note: Reading this book counts as cross-training.]

Susan completed her first ever Parkrun, three loops of the pond at Victoria Park. Arriving home she slumped, exhausted, onto the sofa.

"How was it?" asked her husband handing her a large gin and tonic.

"Awful!" exclaimed Susan, "I was lapped by a three year old pushing her doll in a pram."

"Awww, don't be upset," said her husband in an attempt to comfort her, "she's probably been running for ages."

"What makes it worse," moaned Susan, "she wasn't even taking the race seriously – the wee brat was running in a princess costume!"

A ghost joined our runner club and now enters all our races. He never wins – he just loves the team spirit.

A piece of jigsaw entered the London Marathon. He wasn't a very good runner - he just wanted to be part of something big.

The three bears returned from their morning run.

"Someone's been eating my porridge," said Daddy Bear.

"And someone's been eating my porridge," said Mummy Bear.

"For flup sake stop going on about your stupid porridge," said Baby Bear, "the bastard's gone and nicked my Garmin."

Two Ultra-runners got married – they wanted to have a long distance relationship.

"Alex and I had a massive argument last night," Jane told her friend.

"Why what happened?" asked Kate.

"I hadn't seen him for so long I thought he'd gone off with another woman. Turned out he'd just been out for a long training run," said Jane with a sigh.

"So why the massive argument?" asked Kate.

"Well," said Jane, "by the time he'd got back I'd sold off his car and trashed his record collection.

Gerry was delighted with his special prize at the Boston Marathon – apparently he was the 100,000 runner to DNF

DNF

Doctor: "I'm sorry Mr Knox but I'm afraid you're going to have to stop running."

Patient: "Oh shit! Why?"

Doctor: "Because I'm trying to examine you."

Two lions, Leo and Aquarius, were keen runners so it was no surprise to the other jungle animals when Aquarius announced that he was going to attempt the 156 mile Marathon des Sables.

Leo, being more experienced, promised to help Aquarius train and to support him during the race.

Aquarius trained hard and, true to his word, Leo was always there giving him encouragement and advice. On long run days Leo and Aquarius would run together and Leo would repeatedly emphasize the need for carbo-loading.

Come the first day of the race, Leo was with his friend at the start. "Remember – if you're going to complete this race you will need to regularly carbo-load so you have enough energy," he repeated many times.

At the half way point Leo was there to cheer Aquarius on but was worried when he saw him looking sluggish and tired.

"Carbo-loading!" he called out as his friend went by. "Keep carbo-loading!"

Aquarius stopped dead, looked round at Leo and said angrily, "if I have to eat one more bloody runner you're going to have to carry me over the finish line!"

FunRunFact: Legging It

Rab Lee and Mark Howlett hold the Guinness World Record for the longest distance run three legged in 24 hours. At the Glenmore 24 Hour Trail Race, in the Cairngorms National Park, Scotland, on 7-8 September 2013 the pair managed a staggering 109.8km.

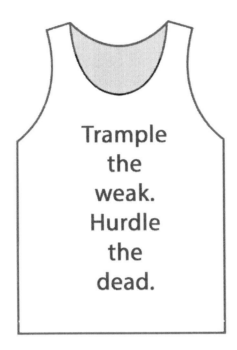

Trample
the
weak.
Hurdle
the
dead.

Runner's Dictionary:
Kit
All you need to run is a pair of cheap trainers. That's what all the magazines say. Nonsense!
The truth is, for most runners, buying all the expensive kit means making small sacrifices elsewhere in their lives – including re-mortgaging the house, selling the car and putting the kids up for adoption.

DNF
"Did Not Finish" is to runners what "Macbeth" is to actors – words that must never be uttered. To avoid using these awful words runners use the abbreviation DNF - which is a little less painful to admit.

Pacer

Pacers are used as a measure of your failure in a race. Standing at the start line you are full of optimism and set out with the 3:30 pacer. Before long the 4:00, 4:30 and 5:00 pacers have drifted by and you spend the last part of the race desperately trying to keep going so the Sweeper doesn't make you take the Numpty Bus.

PB

Personal Best is the utopia of running. It is the thought of achieving a new PB that gets us all up on cold, wintry days to plod the roads and trails for hour after hour. It is why we enter twenty races every single year and cover over 2000 miles in training. It is the dream that is always just one more race away – just one more tweak to the training plan. For the average runner their last PB was 7 years and 3 months ago.

Carbo-Loading

This is the science of fuelling the body to ensure optimum performance in a race. In reality it means that for four weeks before and after a race we can allow ourselves to pig out on burgers, chips, pizzas, chocolate and beer by evoking the golden excuse, "It's okay - I'm carbo-loading."

Physiotherapists

The faith healers of the running world. Physiotherapy is an art rather than a science – and a very abstract art at that! The main strategy physiotherapists employ is to have you perform pointless exercises for weeks during which time your injury has the chance to repair itself naturally.

Cross-Training

An excuse used by runners when they can't be bothered going out for a run. A typical use of the term being; "I'm not doing a long run today. I'm cross-training by sitting watching a three hour long Star Wars movie while drinking copious amounts of Prosecco and downing a dozen doughnuts – Result!!!"

Shoes
Running shoes are very expensive – often costing as much as £150. However, runners should not feel that they are being ripped off. Breaking down the cost we find: £1:50 for materials, £0:13 to have the bits stitched together by some 11 year old Vietnamese kid, £50 to the retailer and £98:87 to have a shiny, brand logo attached to the side. The shiny logo is the most important part of the shoe for it is having the right logo that gives you confidence to run faster than the cheapos who turn up at races wearing £2 sandshoes.

Jelly Babies
A treat that runners consume in an effort to convince their brains that what they are doing is actually fun!!

Ultra
A race of seemingly impossible distance that allows finishers lifetime bragging rights and a feeling of smug superiority over mere marathon runners. Example of use: "Now that I'm an Ultra-runner I feel that marathons are a bit like Parkruns – only of use as training runs."

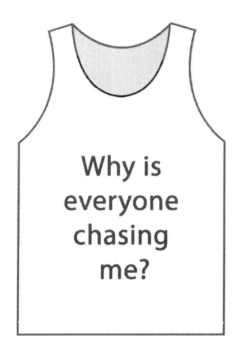

Why is
everyone
chasing
me?

I once had a job where I'd run hundreds of miles in new trainers to test them out. I had to give it up though – it was sole destroying.

As a hobby I taught some herbs how to run. Each week I would challenge them to a race but I always won.
Friends said that I was mad – but I was just ahead of my thyme.

You are a compulsive runner if . . .

* The bib from your favourite race is framed and hangs above the television.
* You named your first-born, Virgin London Marathon.
* You've seen Chariots of Fire thirty-seven times.
* You wear your running kit underneath your work clothes so that you can get going straight after work.
* You know the 5 km point from your house no matter which direction you travel.
* You fall on a trail breaking a leg and the first thing you do is press, 'Stop' on your Garmin.
* Every photo on your Facebook page shows you running.
* You are forty-seven yet still eat jelly babies.
* Your leg muscles have developed muscles of their own.
* Your shoe collection consists of seventeen pairs of expensive trainers and an old pair of moccasins you wear to work, funerals, weddings and all other non-running events.
* You can convert any distance from miles into kilometres without even thinking.
* You often wear clothes which, if you were not in a race, could easily get you arrested.
* You can remember your times for every race you've run, but you can't remember the date of your husband's birthday.
* #YOUNEVERSTOPTWEETINGABOUTRUNNING

Last year, while doing the Loch Ness Marathon, I caught up with a lad who had a car door strapped to his side.

"Why are you running with a car door strapped to your side?" I enquired.

"Because I often get too hot when I'm running," he replied.

"So how does having a car door strapped to your side help?" I asked.

He looked at me as if I was stupid and said, "This way, when I get too hot, I can just wind down the window."

Don't pass
me
I'm not in
your
age group.

The Different Species of Runners:
The Poser: This species of runner wears expensive, colour co-ordinated running gear or perhaps something distinctive such as tartan shorts and vest. They dress to be noticed rather than for speed. They are at their most entertaining on a race as they approach a camera. Here they instinctively go into 'display mode' leaping into the air as they kick their heels and flap their arms frantically – impersonating the mating dance of the six-plumed bird of paradise. These runners do not enter to win, their trophy is applause – their medal is admiration.

The Social Runner: This category of runner is more likely to be found on Facebook than on the trails. They will have at least one-thousand 'running friends' on social media and will chat for hours every day about races, nutrition and the latest running fads. They may actually enter a couple of races each year so that they have a goal to chat about but frequently they will withdraw at the last moment. They are the race-groupies who endure swarms of viscous midges, gale force winds and torrential rain to act as marshals at races or be part of support teams.

The Speeder: This breed of runner is the type you see on the front line at races wearing their club colours. They are skinny, introverted and determined to win. They set off at a pace that is alien to the average participant and, most annoyingly, they seem to run effortlessly. After the race they will spend an hour analysing every detail of their performance with their personal trainers then load up their race statistics onto a spreadsheet so that learnings can be made before the next race.

The Plodder: This class of runner is the keenest of all the classifications. They are likely to compete in at least twenty races each year – though the term compete is used rather loosely. They are often referred to as the Chatterers or the Backmarkers – to them speed is not important – it is all about 'taking part'. The average Plodder is likely to have completed over 50 marathons or ultra-marathons and will insist on talking about them to anyone who is slow enough to listen. The Plodder is usually well known to the Race Sweeper.

The Middle-of-the-Packer: This is the largest group of runners and at races do the important job of filling the gap between the Speeders and the Plodders. These runners train hard, eat healthily and turn out regularly at races even though they have absolutely no chance of winning. For them the best thing that can happen on a race is that they achieve a Personal Best or, on rare occasions, get a 3rd prize in their Age Category. However, without these runners paying the entry fees and turning up to run there would be no races for the Speeders to win, no races for the Plodders to plod, no races for the Posers to exhibit and no races for the Social Runner to blog about.

The Fancy Dresser: This sub-species of runner is a summer migrant to the racing world. They are most commonly spotted at races where there are very large flocks of runners. Fancy Dressers are easy to detect in the crowd as they are likely to be wearing a hippopotamus, unicorn, fairy or other weird costume rather than the standard running kit worn by other species. Middle-of-the-Pack runners dislike the Fancy Dressers – especially when overtaken by one who is wearing a two-ton Black Panther Tank outfit.

On the start line of the Edinburgh Marathon were two runners wearing fancy dress. One was dressed as a chicken and the other as an egg.
I thought to myself, "This should be interesting."

Signs that you are struggling . . .
* It is only 23 metres since you last checked your Garmin.
* You've thrown away your energy gels and gone in for a Triple Decker Big Mac.
* The Sweeper is so bored waiting for you he's playing Badland on his iPad.
* There are wild celebrations at checkpoints when you finally arrive.
* You are overtaken by an old lady with a zimmer.
* Your support team has given up and gone to the pub.
* You vow that this is absolutely the last time you do a 'Fun Run' at your son's school sports day!

When Abdullah took up jogging, he was astounded by the wide selection of jogging shoes available at the local sports shop. After trying on dozens of pairs he noticed that one pair had a tiny pocket at the side.

"What's this little pocket thing for?" he asked the rather fit looking assistant.

The assistant looked Abdullah up and down contemptuously, sneering at his rotundous stature, "That, good sir, is a pocket just big enough to conceal a £10 note," he said disdainfully, "so that when after five kilometres you discover that you're not a runner you will be able to get a taxi back home."

**Spot the Duck loves Ultras
but
he hates all the hanging about.**

Running books I would love to read . . .
* From Park Runner to Olympic Medallist in 30 days –
You can do it!
* Lose 7 pounds by just reading this book.
* Half your marathon time by doing half as much training.
* Steak Pie recipes that guarantee faster Parkrun times.
* Exercises to do in your sleep.
* Overeat your way to a healthy body.
* Reviewed : Top 10 trainers at under £20.
* The 12 steps to a life free from running.
* Pooh Bear's guide to fartlek.

It was the Paisley Athletics Championships and Zander was favourite to win the 800 metres race. He set out strong but as he ran towards the finish he was hit by a turkey, a Christmas pudding and then a bottle of mint sauce. Furious he stormed up to the organisers complaining that he'd been hampered.

If you ever feel the urge
to try cross country
running, start with a
very small country.

Why did the runner cross the road? To try to keep up with the chicken.

Plodder the Tortoise and Dasher the Hare were having a few beers at the Sole and Heel Country Pub one evening. As usual Dasher was boasting about how fast he could run and rhyming off all the races he'd completed and the amazing times he'd achieved.

Plodder was fed up with the boasting and, bolstered by six pints of strong ale, he made a bet with Dasher that he could cross the finishing line of the 2016 Brighton Marathon less than 4 hours after the race started. The bet was agreed - the wager - two big carrots.

Come the big day Dasher was waiting at the finish line and was amazed to see his friend cross the line in 3 hours 59 minutes. But a bet was a bet so he presented Plodder with two huge, juicy carrots.

Once he got home Plodder's wife made him a special bowl of carrot soup to celebrate his achievement. As he sat with his medal round his neck, sipping his soup, Plodder could not help grinning at having won the bet.

"I don't know why you're looking so smug," chided his wife, "cheating your friend like that."

"I didn't cheat," replied Plodder huffily, "I said I'd cross the line within 4 hours of the race starting and I did."

"Yeah," said his wife coldly, "but you didn't let Dasher know you started out with last year's runners."

I'm really amazed at my seventy year old grandmother. She's a fabulously, inspirational woman.

She has run at least 10 kilometres every day since she took up running at the age of sixty-five.

My grandfather's not too happy about it though – he's just had to pay her fare back from Australia.

"Do you like my new GPS?" asked David, "It cost me nearly £2000."

"Bloody Hell!" exclaimed Wilson, "That's expensive!"

"Ah, but it's got an Emergency Button," said David.

"Wow! That could be useful," said Wilson. "How does it work?"

"Simple," said David, "press this big red button and it guides you to the nearest pub."

How do you get fifty runners into a telephone box?
Chuck in a handful of jelly babies.

How do you get fifty runners out of a telephone box?
Chuck in a pair of sweaty trainers!

Tell my
loved ones
that
I tried
my best.

Things you probably won't hear on a marathon . . .
* Fancy dress? This? No, I'm on my way to my wedding.
* There was no queue for the toilets.
* Was that the twenty mile marker? I didn't think we'd even done twelve!
* I wish I hadn't trained so much.
* The Beer and Donut Station is coming up soon.
* If you're not busy later would you like to join me for a wee 10 miler?
* After you.
* Actually I've never run before, I just came out for a pint of milk.
* This is not a costume – I really am a Unicorn!
* So . . . is a marathon more than a 10k?

Why did the runner cross the road? He thought it was a Vampire.

The Four Ages of Running
At 18 to 34: Compete.
At this age we go along to a race with hopes of winning. Or, to be slightly more precise, we go along to a race hoping that none of the good runners are there so we have a slim chance of being in the top ten.

At 35 to 49: Participate.
The golden age of running. We now have no aspirations of winning - all we want to do is occasionally get a Personal Best – even if this means entering new races of odd distances – such as the 3.36km Wind Assisted Downhill Trail Race. We have now also accumulated a whole array of excuses for Bad-Race-Days . . . "I can't go fast with this dodgy knee.", "Oh my plantar fasciitis is fair acting up today!" and, of course, there is the often heard cry of, "I'm just bloody crap at running."

At 50 to 64: Persevere.
By this age we have given up all hope of being fast in shorter distance races and console ourselves that what we lack in speed we now make up for in perseverance. We gravitate towards ultra-marathons where, during a race, it is quite acceptable to walk 'a little' or stop somewhere scenic for a three course meal. Our target now is to finish five minutes before the race time limit without having a coronary.

At 65 to 78¾ : Glory
At this age we get unfettered hero-worship just for finishing a race – even if it's a 1km Santa Run in which we manage to collapse over the line in 2 hours 17 minutes.

After completing the London Marathon, Angela was driving home through the night to Inverness. By seven o'clock in the morning she had reached Glasgow but was feeling exhausted.

Near Glasgow Green she dozed off and almost crashed into a lamppost. She decided to pull onto the side of the road for a short rest.

She turned off the engine, closed her eyes and quickly drifted off to sleep.

A few minutes later an old man in a bright blue running jacket knocked on her window, scaring her half to death.

"Sorry to wake you love," he said breathlessly. "But can you tell me what time it is?"

Angela glanced at her watch. "7:15," she said rather abruptly.

The old man thanked her and ran off.

"Just my luck," she muttered. "I'm parked on some idiot's jogging route."

With a sigh, she settled back into her seat and tried to get back to sleep.

Within minutes two male runners in their twenties knocked on her window. If she hadn't been so tired, she might have found them cute. Now, they were just plain annoying.

"Hi," the blond jogger said.

"Do you have the time?" his brown-haired friend asked.

Angela sighed and looked at her watch. "7:19," she grumped.

"Thanks," they said as they jogged off.

Angela looked down the road and saw more joggers coming her way. Irritated, she found a pen in her bag and scrawled 'I DO NOT KNOW THE TIME' on the back of a running magazine. She put the hastily constructed sign in the rear window and settled back to sleep.

A short time later an old jogger knocked on the window just as she started to doze off.

Angela pointed at the sign and shouted, "Can't you read?"

"Sure I can, miss." he replied politely. "I just wanted to let you know, it's 7:25."

I went to my local sports shop recently to buy a new pair of trainers. I asked Giovanna, the assistant, if there were any technological innovations I should be aware of.

"Yeah," he replied, "there's a brilliant new pair that can forecast the weather."

"Wow," I said, "that's amazing, how do they work?"

"You leave them outside overnight," replied Giovanna, "in the morning if they are wet it's raining. If they are dry it's sunny. If you cannot see them it's foggy. If they are white it's snowing. If they are no longer there it's either windy some bugger has nicked them".

How many ultra-runners does it take to change a light bulb? 35.

22 in hi-vis jackets to point the way to the light, 12 to provide sustenance and encouragement along the journey and 1 to DNF while attempting to change the bulb.

Bricklayer
Runner
I just
hit
the wall.

FunRunFact: Randy Runners

Running boosts your sex drive. Just two and a half hours of running each week increases testosterone levels by 15% in men. Women experience arousal and enhanced orgasm due to increased blood circulation. Yeah – your testosterone levels are high – but you're just too exhausted to do anything about it!

Songs You Do Want to Hear When Running:
* Born to Run - Bruce Springstein
* Running Fast - The Meters
* I Don't Wanna Stop - Ozzy Osbourne
* Running Free - Iron Maiden
* Beautiful Day - U2
* Run, Baby, Run - Sheryl Crow
* I am a winner - Mr. Flipper
* Run to the Hills - Iron Maiden
* Long Distance Runner - Fugazi.
* Ready, Steady, Go - The Meices
* Running Down a Dream - Tom Petty
* The Running Kind - Johnny Cash
* Marathon - Rush
* We Are the Champions – Queen
* All I do is Win - DJ Khaled
* Long May You Run - Neil Young
* The Winner Takes it All – ABBA
* Harder Better Faster Stronger - Daft Punk
* Ready to Run - Dixie Chicks
* Heart of a Champion – Nelly

Two vultures are sitting on a pole watching the Great Scottish 10k race.

"Let's eat that runner in the bright pink leggings," says the first vulture.

"Nah," replies the second vulture.

Ten minute later the first vulture says, "I'm hungry. Can I eat that runner with the luminous green vest?"

"Nah," replies the second vulture.

Twenty minutes later the first vulture pleads, "Oh come on - let's eat a runner before I starve to death."

"Be patient," chided the second vulture, "all the juiciest ones are at the back."

Philosophy of Running:
* I run therefore I am. I am therefore I run.
* Death before DNF.
* I overtrain so I can overeat.
* Should I collapse, please pause my Garmin.
* I have the courage to start, the strength to endure and the resolve to finish.
* Run – eat – sleep – repeat.
* I run with my heart 'cos my legs are shit.
* Running is a mental sport – we are all insane.
* I took the road less travelled . . . and got bloody well lost!
* Born to run – forced to work.
* The faster I run the sooner I eat.
* What's the point!!!!

What do Ultra-runners do for a warmup?
A marathon!
What do Marathon-runners do for a warmup?
A 10k.
What do 10k-runners do for a warmup?
A Parkrun.
What do Parkrunners do for a warmup?
Have an extra couple of hours in bed.

Songs You Don't Want to Hear When Running:
* Train in Vain - The Clash
* Shoot the Runner - Kasabian
* Tired of Running - Snoop Lion
* Running on Empty - Jackson Browne
* Runnin' Blue - The Doors
* Another one bites the dust- Queen
* Bad Runner - Brodinski
* I'm Lost - Runnerz
* Running out of Pain -12 Stones
* Lost and Running - Powderfinger
* Sad Run - City Hunter
* Lost Race - The McMash Clan
* Loneliness of the Long Distance Runner - Iron Maiden
* Gonna Make You Sweat - C+C Music Factory
* I'm Still Standing - Elton John
* Kick Start My Heart - Motley Crue
* Running Scared - Roy Orbison
* Joker On The Run – Spirit
* 'Till I Collapse – Eminem

"Come on lads let's have a race," said Jesus.
"No way," said Paul, "you always cheat."
"I do not," said Jesus indignantly.
"Yes you do," said Peter, "last time we raced you ran across the river leaving the rest of us standing on the bank."
"And the time before that," added Judas, "you turned our isotonic drinks into wine – we got so blotto we couldn't keep up."

When I took up running I could hear clapping from behind me every time I went out for a run. It took me a month to realize that it was my bum cheeks cheering me on.

Lorna loved to run, in fact she ran so much that her husband became worried it was becoming an obsession. He noticed a sign on the local Community Hall for a Jogoholics Anonymous Group that met at 3pm every Sunday afternoon. After a lot of coaxing Lorna eventually agreed to go along.

So, at precisely 3pm, Lorna turned up and the Community Hall only to discover the place was empty.

She sat on the steps outside the hall wondering what to do. A few minutes later she heard whistling and, from around the side of the building, the caretaker appeared.

"Where are all the people for Jogoholics Anonymous?" asked Lorna.

"Oh you'll not find any of them here today love, they're all away," said the caretaker cheerfully, "today's the group's monthly marathon."

Health and Safety
made me
give up running.
My thighs kept rubbing
together
setting fire to my shorts.

**Sometimes Spot the Duck
just can't decide
which way to run.**

It was the AGM of the Jungle Running Club and the committee was discussing who should be awarded the prestigious "Runner of the Year" award.

"Yiannis the Lion has won it for the last nine years. We need to give it to him," said Dean.

"But he hasn't won a race all season," said Scott.

"Yeah that's right," agreed Pyllon, "our newest member has won every single race."

After forty minutes of heated debate, Dod, the chairman, called for a vote. The result was almost unanimous, twenty of the members voted for the newcomer and only Dean voted for Yiannis."

After the meeting, as they drank a few beers, Dod sat down beside Dean and said, "you're not happy that the Runner of the Year award has gone to a newcomer, are you?"

"It's not the fact that he's a newcomer that bothers me," said Dean reflectively, "I just don't understand how he always wins so easily. I've never once seen Sergio the Cheetah do any training!"

Lee was standing on the start line of the Blackpool Marathon chatting to another runner.

"I ran here all the way from Aberdeen," said Lee smugly.

"Bloody Hell," said the amazed runner, "you must be super keen."

"Not really," replied Lee, "the train fare would have cost me a whopping £42.78."

I went into a cheap sports shop and picked up a pair of luminous pink trainers. Immediately the assistant was by my side to see if I needed help.

"Can you tell me if these are for over-pronators?" I asked.

"No, madam," replied the assistant cheerfully, "they're for runners."

I run
because walking
is way too
pedestrian.

"We had a newcomer to the club last night. He wasn't very smart," said Rab to his running friend. "Would you believe he said to the trainer, 'If I run faster than the speed of sound will I still be able to hear my iPod?'"

"What an idiot," said Clare, "No beginner's group would ever be going that fast!"

Things you don't want to hear a race marshal say . . .
* Sorry mate, we packed up six hours ago.
* You'll laugh at this . . . we forgot to bring the drop-bags.
* It's uphill for the next thirty-two miles.
* Which way? To be honest I'm not sure.
* Come in number twenty-three your time is up.
* We messed-up – the route's actually twelve miles longer than we thought.
* Be careful there are hungry wolves on the next section.
* Shit! We've run out of medals.
* There's severe thunder storms and gale force winds on the hills ahead – might be worthwhile saying a wee prayer.

Come on
guys
it doesn't
hurt to
cheer.

Park Runners - Sprint.
10k Runners - Speed.
Marathoners - Strive.
Ultra-runners - Plan their next meal.

Old runners never die,
they just become
quicker and quicker . . .
at DNFing.

Peter was running through Glasgow Green early one
winter's morning when he spotted a down-and-out sleeping
on a bench. Peter slowed down to have a look at him. He
was a young lad in his mid-twenties who looked as if he
hadn't had a decent meal for weeks. He was wrapped in a
filthy, thin blanket that did little to protect him from the
sub-zero wind that was blowing through the park. Peter felt

sorry for him and, remembering the emergency £10 he always carried when running, he decided to give it to the young lad.

Hesitantly Peter went up to him and shook him gently.

"Go away ya bastard!" shouted the down-and-out. "Leave me a-fucking-lone."

"Hey bud," said Peter softly. "Sorry to wake you but I wanted to give you some money."

"Oh right mate," said the down-and-out. "Sorry tae shout at ye like that but thon polis keep moving me oan."

Peter discovered that the down-and-out was called Tosh. He was twenty-three and had been living on the streets since he was fifteen. Tosh was very grateful for the £10 and thanked Peter profusely. After chatting for a few minutes Peter ran on, happy that he was able to help someone less fortunate.

A week later Peter was running through the park again and spotted Tosh sitting on a bench.

"How ya doing bud?" enquired Peter cheerfully.

"Look, look," gasped Tosh, excitedly, pointing at the pair of trainers he was wearing, "I didnae spend yon money oan booze. I went tae the charity shop and got shoes just like yours."

Peter was very impressed and, as he was carrying his wallet that day, he gave Tosh £20.

It was another two weeks before Peter returned to the park. This time Tosh spotted him and came hurrying eagerly towards him.

"Look at me," he yelled pulling his moth eaten coat to the side, "I bought maself a pair of shorts wae yon money."

"Wow!" replied Peter. "You're looking great."

The pair of them chatted for twenty minutes and Tosh asked Peter all sorts of questions about running and races. Before leaving, Peter took £50 from his wallet and gave it to his new 'friend'. He was thrilled that Tosh was looking healthier and didn't seem to be quite so under the influence of the booze. Peter smiled as he ran home, feeling a little smug that maybe his kindness was having a positive effect.

As winter turned to spring Peter ran in the park more frequently but, although he always watched out for Tosh, he was disappointed not to see him again.

It was two years later that Peter completed the Ultra Trail du Mont-Blanc. By then he had almost forgotten about Tosh and, as he sat at prize giving waiting to receive his coveted medal, his thoughts were still on the race and the thrill of completing such an amazing challenge.

"But, as the main prizes were being awarded, Peter was jolted out of his thoughts when he heard the race director announce, ". . . and first prize goes to an incredible runner from Scotland . . . Tosh MacDuff."

Peter stared up at the stage as a young athlete went forward to receive the gold medal. He was a strong, lean lad wearing expensive clothes. He slightly resembled the down-and-out that Peter had befriended. For a moment Peter thought it was him and he couldn't help but chuckle slightly at such a ridiculous notion.

Tosh heard Peter's chuckles and looked down from the stage. He instantly recognized Peter. Tosh ran across the stage, leapt down and continued running towards Peter.

"Ya bastard!" he yelled. "Ya fucking bastard – I'm gonnae kill you."

He threw himself at Peter, lashing out with his fists. It took four big guys to restrain him but he continued with his verbal assault on Peter.

"What have I done?" asked Peter, shocked at what was happening, "I only ever tried to help you."

"You ruined everything mate. Everything. My life used to be simple. I had a wee drink. I chatted with mates. I had another wee drink. I got some kip. That was it. Simple. Relaxed. Nae problems," shouted Tosh, still being held back from hitting Peter. "And then you came along planting ideas intae ma head and the next thing I knew I was hooked on running. Oh, it started out with just 10ks but then I progressed to half-marathons and then marathons – before I knew it I was into the real hard stuff - doing ridiculously long ultra-marathons."

"But you're obviously an amazing athlete," said Peter nervously, "and that's fantastic."

"No it bloody well isn't," screamed Tosh, "Now I have to get up at 6am every day and run a huge number of miles. Now I have to travel all over the world to compete in more and more challenging races. And do you know what is really shit – now I have to work! I have to work 60 hours a fucking week to afford this stupid addiction."

Tears of exasperation streamed down Tosh's face as he thought of the lifestyle he had lost.

"You bastard!" he cried in despair, "Why did you do this to me? Why did you ruin ma life?"

FunRunFact: Long Way for a Jog

Longest Ultramarathon : Since 1997, runners have been competing in the Self-Transcendence 3100 Mile Race, which is billed as the longest official footrace in the world. They run 100 laps a day for up to 50 days around a single block in Queens, NY, for a total distance of 3,100 miles (5,000 km). The 2015 winner was Ashprihanal Aalto, of Helsinki Finland who completed the distance in 40 days+09:06:21 to achieve a world record.

It's time to hang up your trainers if you're overtaken by any of the following:

* Gila Monster (Speed: 0.4 miles per hour)
* Slug (Speed: 0.2 miles per hour)
* Giant Tortoise (Speed: 0.17 miles per hour)
* Three Toed Sloth (Speed: 0.15 miles per hour)
* Snail with a sore head (Speed: 0.05 miles per hour)
* Coral Reef (Speed: 0 miles per hour)

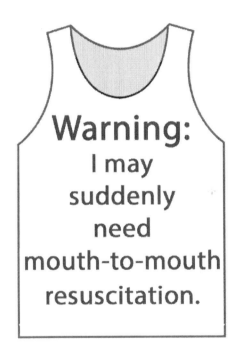

Warning: I may suddenly need mouth-to-mouth resuscitation.

I'm a bit self-conscious wearing shorts when running as I have flabby thighs. Fortunately my massive stomach covers them quite nicely.

One day while out for his morning jog, Ian noticed a tennis ball lying by the side of the pavement. Being fairly new and in good condition, he picked it up, put it in his pocket and proceeded on his way. A few minutes later another runner came towards him and noticed the large bulge.

"What's that big lump you have?" he asked.

"Tennis ball," replied Ian breathlessly.

"Wow," said the man, "running with that must hurt. I once had tennis elbow and the pain was unbearable!"

It was 20:55 when George arrived at the door of the prestigious Toffs in Tails Hotel where the prize giving was due to take place. The doorman, wearing his distinctive red tuxedo, eyed George up and down suspiciously as he approached the entrance.

"Where are you going sir?" he asked George politely but firmly.

"Darnhard 100 Mile Ultra Prize Giving," replied George impatiently, "winner come to collect his gold medal"

"Not in that track suit and trainers you're not," said the doorman snidely.

"But I won the race," said, George brusquely, "they can't have prize giving without me!"

"I see," said the doorman pensively, "so, if you won, you must be a pretty fast runner?"

"Yes, one of the fastest ultra-runners on the planet," replied George irritably.

"Well in that case you'll have no problem running to your grubby little hotel and coming back wearing something more appropriate," chided the doorman.

I was going to get up early and go jogging, but my toes voted against me 10 to 1.

Some Rather Strange Races:
Man versus Horse Marathon
The Man versus Horse Marathon is an annual race over 22 miles, where runners compete against riders on horseback. The race, which is slightly shorter than an official marathon, takes place in the Welsh town of Llanwrtyd Wells every June. In 2004, the 25th race was won by Huw Lobb in 2 hours, 5 minutes and 19 seconds. It was the first time that a man racing on foot has won the race, thereby winning the prize fund of £25,000.

Cupid's Undies Race
Since its conception in 2009 this strange race has grown in popularity and is now held in almost forty cities across the USA every Valentine's Day. Although just one mile long there is a catch – the dress code states that you must run in your undies. All fine you may think– except that often in

February there can be several feet of snow at some of the locations! Brrrrrrrr!!! Brass Monkeys!!!

Piece of String
Described by the organisers as "The World's most pointless race" the Piece of String is run over a random distance decided by the organisers at some arbitrary point during the race. The 2013 event was around 130 miles. Perhaps because of the uncertainty over distance, there is a very high drop-out rate – usually between twelve and fifteen start the race but, on average, only two manage to finish.

North American Wife Carrying Championship
Although not over a great distance – the course is a mere 254 meters – runners are slightly hampered by the need to carry their wives and having to negotiate an obstacle course filled with log hurdles, sand traps, and water hazards. Interestingly one of the rules is that, "All participants must enjoy themselves."

Empire State Building Run Up
The Empire State Building Run-Up is the world's oldest and most famous tower race. For the past 38 years, runners from around the globe have gathered to race up its famed 86 flights of 1,576 stairs. While visitors can reach the building's Observatory by elevator in under a minute, the fastest runners cover the 86 floors in about 10 minutes.

Bay to Breakers
Bay to Breakers is an annual race in San Francisco. It has been run for more consecutive years than any other footrace in the world. The phrase "Bay to Breakers" reflects the fact that the race starts at the northeast end of the downtown area near the Embarcadero and runs west through the city to finish at the Great Highway (adjacent to the Pacific coast, where breakers crash onto Ocean Beach).

The complete course is 7.46 miles long. It is famous for participants wearing flamboyant costumes, and even more for the runners who don't bother to wear anything at all!! Just think – no chaffing. ☺

Bisbee Ice-Man
A very odd race held each year in Bisbee, Arizona. It was created to honour the men who once delivered blocks of ice by hand before the advent of refrigeration. Competitors have to grab a 10 pound block of ice using a pair of antique tongs. They then sprint up 155 stairs, run across a trail that takes them back to the paved road then rush down a steep winding hill to the finish. Cool!

The Three Most Troublesome Running Injuries:
Plantar Fasciitis

Plantar fasciitis is an inflammation in the bottom of the foot, and is one of the biggest problems that plagues the running wounded. Sufferers feel a sharp, tight, painful sensation at the base of the heel that can be excruciating. Often during a race you will hear the cry, "Oh shit, my Plantar Fasciitis is fair killing me."

Runner's Knee

A mysterious pain that comes on suddenly whenever you consider going for a training run. Strangely the pain disappears immediately you abandon thoughts of training and head for the pub. Sometimes called Old Codger's Knee as it tends to mainly affect older runners – i.e. those over the age of twenty-three.

Lazyfatbastarditis

This debilitating condition affects most runners at some stage. It is the main excuse given for skipping a training session and for causing runners to DNF. Sufferers find that regularly consuming a massive curry and three bottles of prosecco does nothing to improve the condition but they live in hope that one day it will.

If you're behind me you've probably timed-out!

A blonde goes out for a run around the streets of Glasgow. She comes to the River Clyde and wants to cross but can't see a bridge nearby. Luckily she spots another blonde runner on the opposite bank.

"Yoohoooo doll!" she shouts, "How do I get to the other side?"

Somewhat confused the second blonde looks up the river then down the river. After some careful thought she shouts back, "You're already on the other side honey!"

**Being of small stature,
Spot the Duck
finds running can
be a dangerous
pastime!**

Gordon bet his wife, Patricia, that she couldn't run up and down Ben Nevis. It took her six hours but she did it and Gordon had to buy her an expensive pair of shoes. The following week he bet her that she couldn't improve on her time. She did and he had to buy her a new gold watch. This continued for several weeks – each time Patricia would improve on her time – and each time Gordon would have to buy her an expensive gift.

One day Patricia was proudly showing off the new iPad that Gordon had just bought her.

"You're an eejit," said her friend, "you just don't get what's going on!"

"What do you mean?" asked Patricia.

"Each week while you're killing yourself running," explained the friend, "your husband is having it off with the woman that lives in the cottage at the foot of the Ben."

Things you may hear on a marathon . . .
* God this is tough – have we reached 500 metres yet?
* I only do this to get some 'me' time.
* I've just hit the wall. Damn – what a dumb place to build a bloody wall.
* Fun runner? No – I'm actually a sadomasochist.
* I didn't start running until I was 73. Sorry, I can't chat longer, I'm trying to catch up with my Dad.
* Knit one purl one, knit one purl one . . . damn I've dropped a stitch.
* What? Is this not the Pollock Parkrun?
* I've found the perfect isotonic drink . . . Guinness.

Two mice, Fasta and Slowa,were out for a jog one morning and found a huge piece of cheese lying on the path.

"It's mine," cried Slowa.

"No, mine," said Fasta.

"Mine, mine mine," said Slowa.

"Okay, let's decide this with a 100 metre race," suggested Fasta.

So they both dashed off as fast as their little legs would carry them. But when they got back, puffing and panting, to the cheese it was a dead heat and impossible to decide a winner.

"Okay, let's try 500 metres," said Slowa.

So they set off again, but once more it was impossible to decide the winner.

"Let's do this properly," said, Fasta, "let's race over 50 miles – first back gets all the cheese."

It was agreed and they set off again running as fast as they could. After 10 miles Slowa was slightly in the lead but he took cramp in his tail and over the next 5 miles Fasta gradually caught up and overtook his friend. But just a few miles later he had to have a toilet stop and once more Slowa got ahead. Fasta dug deep and with just 50 metres to go he took the lead and won the race.

"Well done," said Norunna the Fox as he watched the two mice finish their race, "Had you got back sooner I would have happily given you guys a share of the huge cheese I found."

Moral of this story: If you are a long distance runner, don't leave your cheese lying on the path – especially if there is a greedy fox around.

Race Marshal's biggest lies . . .
* It's all downhill from here.
* You're looking good!
* There's absolutely no way you can get lost.
* I wish I was running this too.
* You're in the lead.
* It's a very quiet road – there are never any cars about.
* Not far to go now.

Bob and Shaun are taking part in a jungle marathon in Africa. After 30km they realise they are being followed by a lion.

"Shit," exclaims Shaun, "we're going to be eaten alive and die an excruciatingly painful death."

"Keep calm and keep running," replied Bob.

"What's the point - we're doomed to having our limbs torn from our bodies," cried Shaun

"Think positive," said Bob calmly, "if we do manage to outrun the beast we're definitely on for a PB!"

Runners don't always tell the truth – here's what they really mean . . .

What they say :: What they mean.

* I haven't trained for this marathon. :: I've been doing more than 80 miles a week for the last 20 weeks.

* I've only entered for fun. :: If I don't win I'm going into a serious sulk for 6 months.

* I'm running for charity. :: I bought all my running gear from Oxfam.

* You look fantastic! :: Christ, you look like a stuffed turkey in those yellow leggings!

* I'm just going to take it easy today. :: Shit, now that I'm forty I'm finding this so difficult.

* Everyone's a winner. :: I just hope I'm not last.

* The crowd really kept me going. :: Bloody Hell – I was terrified I'd get mugged going through that slum.

* This is absolutely, definitely my last long race. :: I wonder if there's a marathon somewhere next week.

* Running helped me lose 2 stones. :: With the cost off all the kit I can't afford to eat.

* I'm going to join the 100 Marathon Club. :: Only 99½ marathons to go.

Long distance runners Troy and Kilian had been adversaries for many years. They disliked each other intensely and, when competing in the same race, each was always eager to beat each other.

One such race was the prestigious 100 mile Hardknock 100 – a race both runners were always desperate to win.

The first time they both competed in it was 2012. Troy set out fast and Kilian struggled to keep up with him and remained behind him for the duration of the race. But with just 500 metres to go Kilian dug deep, upped his pace, and started to overtake his rival. As Kilian went past, Troy shoved him hard and he fell into the rocks at the side of the path. Troy went on to win the race and Kilian hobbled painfully into second place. Afterwards Troy apologised to Kilian for pushing him but explained that he had saved him from a deadly snake that was about to strike.

During the 2013 race the exact same thing happened. 500 metres from the finish Kilian tried to overtake Troy but was pushed to the ground. Again Troy apologised and repeated his claim that he had saved Kilian from a poisonous snake.

At the 2014 race Kilian was determined that the same thing wouldn't happen again so he set out as fast as he could and got an early lead over Troy and all the other runners. However, as he got close to the finish he began to tire and became aware that Troy was catching up. With 500 metres to go Troy drew level. Kilian was about to take revenge and lash out at his rival but at the last moment his conscience got the better of him. However, as Troy hurried past, a snake sprung from the rocks and bit deep into his leg. Kilian froze to the spot, unable to comprehend what had happened.

As he looked on helpless while Troy lay dying an agonizing death the organisers rushed to the scene.

"Damn," said the race director, "It's maybe about time we moved that snake – that's about ten runners it's killed over the last couple of years"

Don't
follow me,
I'm lost
too.

Two lions were sitting at prize giving waiting to receive their West Highland Way Race Goblets.
"I didn't think much of the marshals on this race," moaned the first.
"No," replied the second, "that one at Kinlochleven definitely gave me indigestion."

A flustered man goes to see his doctor, "Doctor, my wife's a runaholic. She's run 50 miles a day for the past 100 days."
"Give her these tablets," said the doctor, "they will fix her out."
"How can I do that?" asked the man indignantly, "she's 5,000 miles away!

"Doctor, I keep thinking I'm a dog," barked the patient in tight leggings.
"Oh dear, how long has this been going on?" asked the doctor.
"Ever since my owner entered me in my first Canicross 10k" replied the patient.

How can you tell if a friend has ran a marathon?
Don't worry, they'll soon tell you. Then tell you again and again and again . . .

An orange was doing his very first marathon but sadly had to drop out after 20 miles – he'd run out of juice.

A lemon came last in the Fruit Category of the Groceries Marathon – he was really bitter.

My doctor told me that jogging could add years to my life. He was right. I've only been running a few weeks and already I feel ten years older.

An ultra-runner goes into the doctor's surgery wearing his shorts and tight vest.
"Doctor you must help me," he said, "I can't stop running."
"Take some of this Imodium," said the doctor, "that should give your bum a rest."

A banana was running the Paris marathon but, much to the amusement of the spectators, it slipped on a person, skint its knees, and had to withdraw.

What do you get if you cross a piece of wood and a very fast runner?
A splinter.

What do you call a Saturday morning 5k run in the park for dogs?
A Bark Run.

What's orange and can run 100 metres in 9.17 seconds?
A carrot on anabolic steroids.

What's green and can run 100 metres in 9.16 seconds?
A lettuce on organic anabolic steroids.

What do you get if you cross a sheep and a hurdler?
A wooly jumper.

FunRunFact: Bushed Out
President George W. Bush ran the Houston marathon in
1993 in 3 hours, 44 minutes.

**Things you never want to hear your Fitness Coach
say . . .**
* Sure I'll take you on. I enjoy a difficult challenge.
* This is going to hurt.
* Was that you running your fastest? I thought you were
doing a penguin impersonation!
* Have you considered taking up golf?
* Technically you're dead.
* Let's start with a gentle forty miler.
* Welcome to my remedial group.
* Don't worry, if need be I can give you CPR.

At the start of the race the organizer was explaining that it was an out-and-back race.

"Where to?" ask one of the runners.

"To here of course," replied the organizer.

Alastair was doing the Dundee Marathon and spotted a rather plump man running along the road carrying a 50 inch television. Catching up with him Alastair exclaimed enthusiastically, "You're amazing mate, what charity are you running for?"

"Don't be such a stupid prick," the man replied without slowing down. "I'm not doing the marathon. I've just nicked this telly."

"Doctor you need to help me," said Mike, "my wife's obsessed with running. Every single Saturday she has to do the local Parkrun. Please tell her to stop."

"But getting exercise is a good thing," replied the Doctor, "why would you want to stop her running?"

"Because every single week she beats me," said Mike.

Why did the farmer race his cow around the field before milking it?
He wanted to have a milk shake.

Two teams of cakes competed in the 4 x 400 race at the Bakery Olympics – which team won?
The Battonbergs.

One team of cakes won all the trophies at the Bakery World Championships . . .
The Cup Cakes.

John from Leeds was voted 'meanest runner of 2015'. He hopped round the Yorkshire Marathon because he was only willing to buy one trainer until he was sure he wanted to take running up seriously.

Did you hear about the stocking that got disqualified from the Edinburgh to London Walking Race – it was caught running.

What's the fastest cake in the marathon?
. . . scone . . .

What noodle overtakes you in the marathon?
. . . . . . pasta . . .

"Doctor, my left knee gets sore every time I run," moaned Bill.
"I'm afraid it's just old age setting in," replied the doctor.
"It can't be that," said Bill indignantly, "my right knee doesn't get sore and it's the exact same age."

Why did Ruth train by pushing a three wheeled cart?
She wanted to run a barrowthon.

Why did Frank run with a courgette in each hand?
He was training to run a marrowthon.

Why did the jogger cross the road?
It was the chicken's day off.

Marathoner's Motto:
If at first you don't succeed,
try, try, try a 10k.

Two flies were training, running laps around the edge of a
saucer but were clearly struggling to get up a decent pace.
"You guys had better get your act together for tomorrow,"
said their coach.
"Why's that ?" they asked.
"Because tomorrow's the annual championships," said the
coach sternly, " and you guys are running in the cup.

You know you're married to a runner if:
* He goes away for a dirty weekend and you don't even consider that he might be having an affair.
* Her ideal family day out is all of you doing a Parkrun.
* 6am is a long lie in.
* You don't recognize his friends with their clothes on.
* She has a database of all her running gear.
* By coincidence, whenever you go on holiday there just happens to be a marathon there.
* He never goes out without a foil blanket, a whistle and an emergency £20.
* Night cramps are the norm.
* You give her a Sweatshop voucher for Valentine's Day and she actually think it's romantic.
* He gets monthly deliveries of Isotonic Drinks from the Wine Club.

Roseanne was disappointed that her first London Marathon took 12 hours but was delighted with the Christian Louboutin python sandals and the Lana Marks alligator handbag she managed to pick up during the little shopping detours she took along the way.

Allan was standing nervously awaiting the start of his very first Parkrun when another runner pointed at his feet and said, "excuse me mate but you've got your trainers on the wrong feet."
Allan stood confused for a moment then replied, "don't be silly – these are the only feet I have."

Tom wore a barcode costume when he ran the New York Marathon. Unfortunately, after 10 miles, he passed a runner dressed as a barcode reader and had to pay $67.34.

Emma joined the Hokey Cokey Running Club but became very frustrated at the length of time it took them to get ready for training runs. They would start with their shorts, put the right foot in, the right foot out. In, out, in, out . . . and the shaking all about went on forever.

Holly and Copper were running together in the Caterpillar Cabbage Patch Race when a butterfly flew overhead. "Bloody Hell," exclaimed Holly, "that bugger surely must be cheating."

Lois completed the 53 mile Highland Fling pushing her 6 month old son all the way in a buggy.
But her celebrations were cut short when the race organisers told her she was being disqualified.
"Why?" asked an exasperated Lois.
"The rules state quite clearly that pacers are not allowed," explained Johnny the Director, "and that baby was clearly in front of you for the whole of the race."

Janice is marshalling at the Great North Run when she spots a snail crossing the line. She picks it up and throws it as far as she can. Three years later Janice is marshalling again and spots the same snail crossing the line. As Janice goes to pick it up she hears the tiny voice of the snail say, 'So what the hell was that all about?'

Two balls of string had a race – it ended in a tie.

Two cameras had a race – it was a photo finish.

Two knives had a race – one got disqualified for cutting the other one up.

Two cadavers had a race – it was a dead heat.

Two cheetahs had a race – they both won.

Two dyslexic runners had an acre. One now the other slot.

Two cartoon characters had a race – it ended in a draw.

Two philosophers had a race in a forest – did either of them win?

Two optimists had a race – one won but the other had the best run of his life.

Two giraffes had a race – it ended neck and neck.

One and a half runners had a race – one won by a fraction.

Two nuns had a race – the first crossed the finish line and the other blessed it.

Two abbreviations had a race – one got a PB the other DNFed.

Two contrary runners had a race - the loser won and the winner came third.

Two streakers had a race – it was over in a flash.

The Saltire and the Union Jack had a race – but very soon they were both flagging.

Two apples had a race – the Granny Smith pipped the Golden Delicious to the line.

Two religious fanatics had a race – although both ran with banners proclaiming "The End is Nigh" they never reached it.

Two snails had a race – we don't know yet who will win.

Two defeatists had a race – one came last and the other finished behind him.

"I've just done a 26.2 miler!" boasted Donald excitedly.
"Wow! Amazing! I didn't think you were fit enough to run a marathon," said his surprised friend.
"Oh, I didn't run," replied Donald, "I drove. It was a Carathon!"

FunRunFact: In the Beginning

The Boston Marathon is the world's oldest marathon. It was first run in April 1897 (with just 15 runners), inspired by the revival of the marathon for the 1896 Summer Olympics in Athens. It is the oldest continuously running marathon, and the second longest continuously running footrace in North America, having debuted five months after the Buffalo Turkey Trot. Now, around 30,000 take part in the Boston Marathon every year.

Honey the Bee finished the Dublin Marathon.
"Did you enjoy that?" asked her proud husband.
"Yeah," she replied, "it gave me a real buzz."

It was the annual Slug Marathon and Sally Slug-MacSlugface smashed the course record. An enthusiastic Slug-Radio interviewer asked her what was her favourite part of the race.

"I'm not sure," replied Sally thoughtfully, "it was all over so quickly."

Did you hear about the cannibal who entered the Vegetarian Marathon?

He was disqualified for eating Jelly Babies.

Did you hear about the cannibal who won the Clown Marathon?

He complained that all the other runners tasted funny.

Roddy is on the last section of the ninety-five mile West Highland Way Race when he hears a runner in front of him crying.

"Are you okay?" asks Roddy catching up.

"Sorry for the tears," says the runner, wiping his face, "it's just that for the last 10 years my wife joined me for this section. But she passed away so this is the first time I've had to do it on my own."

"That's awful," says Roddy. "Could you not have got a relative or friend to join you?"

The man shakes his head sorrowfully. 'No,' he says, tears streaming down his cheeks, 'they're all at the funeral.'

On a long run Spot the Duck
sometimes needs to
take a power nap.

A man turns up for a 10k race with a roll of tarmac under his arm.
"Why are you carrying a roll of tarmac under your arm?" asks another runner.
"I heard this was a road race," replies the man.

I tried to train my pet snail to run a marathon in under 4 hours but he was very slow. In an attempt to make him faster I removed his shell – but if anything it made him more sluggish.

The Lord looked down and said to Gabriel "come forth and you will receive eternal life."
But Gabriel had skipped a few training sessions and came fifth – so all he got was a stupid plastic finisher's medal.

Anne was 50 miles into the Hardrock 100 mile race when she came across another runner, Russel, lying at the side of the track. Through tears of pain Russel explained that he had been bitten on the bum by a poisonous Coral Snake.
"I'll run to the next checkpoint and get a doctor," promised Anne.
So she ran ten miles as fast as she could but when she got to the checkpoint she discovered that the doctor was dealing with a runner who had suffered a heart attack.
"I can't leave my patient," said the doctor, "but all you have to do is take a knife, cut a little cross where the bite is, suck out the poison and spit it on the ground. After that he'll recover quickly."
Anne ran back to Russel, who was by then in utter agony.
"What did the doctor say?" he cried desperately.
"I'm sorry," said Anne clasping Russel's trembling hands, "he says you're going to die,"

Sarah had planned to run the Rome Marathon dressed as an Italian island.
But friends said to her 'Don't be Sicily'.

My coach said I had to try harder –
I had to go that extra mile.
I did and I won –
but the marathon organisers were rather annoyed
at having to chase after me to present my medal.

I first saw my husband-to-be while I was holidaying in Athens. He ran past me in shorts and vest and I discovered that he was doing the Spartathalon Ultra-marathon. I thought to myself, "Well there's a guy who will go far."

Back in 1966, two sandshoe salesmen were sitting in a seedy bar moaning about how little money there was to be made from selling sandshoes.
"I've got a bit of a crazy get rich quick idea," said the first.

"Right, what's that?" asked the second sceptically.

"Well, you know, running is becoming really popular now," said the first, slowly and thoughtfully, "what if we could persuade runners that they needed to wear special running shoes. And what if we made those shoes really expensive so the runners believed they were getting something that would help them run faster?"

The second salesman sat in silence for a while considering the idea.

"Brilliant," he eventually proclaimed, "and what if we convinced them that they had to replace them every five hundred miles?"

"We'd never get away with it," said the first, "they are surely not that dumb."

"Guess not," sighed the second salesman dreamily, "but a nice idea though!"

I saw this beautiful blonde running in the women's 10k. I ran alongside her and, puffing and panting, I asked if I could have her number. "Sure she said," and she handed me her bib.

I was running the Guernsey Waterfront Marathon dressed as a tangerine and a lady shouted that I looked cute. "Yeah," I replied, "I'm appealing."

Amazingly, at the age of 87, Susan, was still running the London Marathon. She set out when she was 82.

Why do Ultra-runners run so many miles in training? Well each year they burn off enough calories to eat 1000 donuts or drink 1300 pints of beer. Now that's got to be a huge incentive.

Last week a friend and I ran three marathons back to back. Luckily I was the one running forward.

How do you start a Jelly Marathon?
Get set!

How do you start a Tapioca Marathon?
Sago!

I have a wonderful new incentive that helps me finish my training runs. I dangle a bottle of beer 10 inch in front of my face. It works every time.

There's nothing like getting up at 5 a.m, jogging ten miles, and then taking an ice-cold shower. There's nothing like it, so I don't do it.

My approach to marathon running is to build up to it very, very gently. As a starter I've enrolled in a running correspondence course.

I did fifty laps this afternoon. I ate lunch in a revolving restaurant.

If you were a dedicated runner you would be out on the trails rather than reading this dumb book!

Derek met up with his wife immediately after he'd finished his first marathon.

"I've got multiple blisters, shin splints, my quads ache and I think I might need a hip replacement," he moaned.

"Yeah, yeah," replied his wife enthusiastically, "but did you enjoy yourself?"

A Scotsman, an Englishman and an Irishman want to get in to watch the Olympics but they haven't got tickets. After some chat they come up with a plan. The Scotsman picks up a manhole-cover, tucks it under his arm and walks to the gate. "MacCampbell, Scotland," he says, "Discus," and in he walks. The Englishman picks up a length of scaffolding and slings it over his shoulder. "Jenkins-Jones, England," he says, "Pole vault," and in he walks. The Irishman nips into a shop and buys ten pork pies, eight bars of chocolate, four bags of jelly babies and two gallons of water. "O'Really, Ireland," he says, "Ultra-runner."

Three six year olds were boasting about their mums.

"My Mum ran a 10 kilometre race," said the first excitedly.

"That's nothing," said the second, "my Mum ran a marathon."

"Huh, that's rubbish," gloated the third, "My Mum did the Moonwalk and look how far away that is."

What's harder to catch the faster you run?
Your breath.

I did my first marathon in fancy dress. I put on a pair of shorts, a vest and a pair of trainers and pretended to be a runner.

For Daniel, ultra-running was an obsession – often his treadmill gave up before he did.

Lazy Bugger's Marathon Training Schedule:
Monday: Rest Day
Tuesday: Speed Work – 2km at 13% of VO2 Max
Wednesday: Cross Training – watch athletics on television.
Thursday: Hill Work – Look at the beautiful mountains as you run the flat canal path.
Friday: Rest Day
Saturday: Back-to-Back Rest Day
Sunday: Long Run – 5km to local café for a celebratory breakfast.

Spot likes to support fellow
runners by marshalling
at races.

Marathon Plan (for those following the Lazy Bugger's Marathon Training Schedule):

0-10k : Start out slow and steady.

10k-20k : Get slower and less steady.

20k-30k : Impersonate a comatose tortoise with multiple corns.

30k-40k : Hobble . . . limp . . . moan . . . hobble . . . limp . . . moan . . .

40k-42k : Steal zimmer frame from spectator.

Last wee bit: Collapse your way towards the finish, hoping that a good looking runner will carry you across the line and the inevitable video will go viral.

At prize-giving the Race Director said "Everyone's a winner". And that, your Honour, is why I buggered-off with the silver trophy.

A friend of mine runs marathons. He always talks about this "runner's high" that he gets. But he has to go 26 agonising miles to achieve it. That's why I smoke and drink. I get the same feeling from a flight of stairs.

Greg was going on his long training run and his wife offered to help by driving along with his food and spare clothes. Greg started out running in front of the car but soon got tired. So he ran behind the car but that just made him exhausted. So he climbed into the back of the car, had sex with his wife, and wrote it up as cross-training.

"I'm so glad I took up running," said Helen, "Now I run home behind the bus and save £2 a night."
"You should run home behind a taxi," said her husband, "that way you could save £20."

Over a few beers a hillrunner, a trailrunner and a roadrunner were boasting about their running achievements.
"I ran Ben Nevis in under two hours," said the hillrunner smugly.
"I completed the Ultra Trail du Mont-Blanc in under twenty-eight hours," boasted the trailrunner.
But they were all agreed that the greatest achievement was the roadrunner's when he proclaimed, "I ran across the M25 in just fifteen minutes!"

Norman had been a not-very-successful runner for fifty years and died suddenly one day while out on a training run. In accordance with his wishes it was arranged that six members of his running club would run the ten kilometres from his house to the cemetery carrying Norman in his coffin. The runners set out on a cold frosty morning with his wife, Betty, his family and friends following in a procession of cars. It was a narrow hilly road that passed through the glen and it would have been difficult to run even without the burden of a coffin. As they ran round a particularly sharp bend one of the runners fell – the coffin flew forward, tumbled down the steep hill and disappeared into a gorge. The whole procession came to an abrupt halt. "Oh for fuck sake," exclaimed Betty in disbelief, "not another bloody DNF."

Did you hear about the village idiot doing his first marathon?
He got tired after 20 miles so turned around and ran back to the start.

Pauline was on the phone to a running friend.
"I've just completed four marathons on my new treadmill and now I'm on to my fifth," she said breathlessly.
"Why on earth are you doing that you nutter?" demanded her friend.
"Because I can't find the bloody off button," whimpered Pauline.

While we are all running who's looking after the World?

Looking at the results of the 10k race, Yanti was surprised that there were loads of vets in the race yet other professions didn't get a mention.

No! These do not count as cross training:
* Competing in a Pie Eating Marathon.
* Marshalling at a Parkrun.
* Watching the football.
* Dreaming of running.
* Walking to the fridge for more beer.
* Uploading 10,000 race photos onto Facebook.
* Playing Grand Theft Auto for fourteen hours.
* Going on a pub crawl.
* Reading this book (I lied!)

Trail Runner, "Excuse me. Will this path take me to Dundee?"
Farmer, "No son, you'll have to go there yourself."

It was quiz night at the village pub and the Village Running Club's team were sitting with their trainers on their heads. "What's going on with the trainers?" asked one of the Village Butcher's team.
"Oh this," came the reply, "it helps jog our memories."

Must-Buy items in the running shop's sale:
* Trainers that are only one size too small.
* Luminous green vest that has been on the rack for seven years.
* Another six pairs of shorts – you can never have enough.
* Jels that are a mere two months past their use-by date.
* A backup Garmin – just in case!

A jogger runs into a bar.
"Shit," he says rubbing his head, "I didn't realize this was an obstacle race."

Apparently for every mile you run, you add one minute to your life. Brilliant! This means that, when I am 85, I will need to spend an additional four months in a nursing home at £3,000 a month.

Audrey was running the Loch Ness Marathon and had built up a lead she hoped was unassailable.
Around the fifteen mile mark she was surprised to hear heavy footsteps behind her. Looking round she saw a man in dungarees and wellingtons coming towards her at speed. But what was really astonishing was that he had a sheep wrapped around his neck.
"Are you in the race," asked Audrey hoping the answer would be negative.
"No, no lassie," I'm just moving some livestock to another farm.
The pair of them ran on together chatting, though Audrey had difficulty keeping up. After five minutes the farmer upped his pace.
"I'd better hurry on lassie," he called, "I'm trying to catch up with the wife – she's got the bull."

The One True Training Plan
(As used by Lesser Runners)
* Create Training Plan.
* Skip sessions because: Going to pub / Injured / Can't be bothered.
* Eat lots of cakes.
* Drink lots of beer.
* Turn up late for race after heavy night out to discover you've forgotten a few essentials (such as shoes and shorts).
* Run very, very slowly.
* Develop one of the following: Blisters, ITBS, Paranoia, Cramp, Plantar Fasciitis, Nausea, Insomnia.
* Run even slower.
* Vow never to run again - EVER!
* Crawl over the Finish Line.
* Moan to random strangers about how hard the race was.
* Enter another race.
* Repeat indefinitely.

Two ultra-runners become shipwrecked but manage to swim to a tiny island that's just 20ft by 20ft.
"This is crap," complains Jenni, "our racing days are over."
"Not at all," exclaims Ross excitedly, "we can race each other around the island. I reckon that 5000 laps would be fifty miles."
"Yeah right," says Jenni, "and how are we going to manage that without twenty marshals and two support crews?"

An Englishman, an Irishman and a Scotsman were having a race. As they ran past the Welshman standing at the side of the track he shouted angrily at them, "How come I never get included in any of your jokes?"

Being a bit overweight I joined my local running club. They assured me I would lose a stone in 4 months. I went along every single week but didn't lose an ounce. Apparently you have to run too.

I have to run early in the morning while my brain's too tired to figure out what I'm doing.

It was the annual Nudist Fun Run – after two miles Ria moaned to her friend, "this bib really bloody well hurts."

Why did the Nuns enter yet another marathon?
Well it was just a habit really.

Why did the skinny runner jog backwards?
He wanted to gain weight!

Sandra realised that her new relationship wasn't going to satisfy her rather strange fantasies when she discover that Ian's skin tight leggings were not sex-wear.

How do crazy runners get through the forest?
They follow the psycho path.

A runner goes into a bar,
"A pint for me and a whisky for the cheetah," he gasps.
"Cheetah? What cheetah?" asks the bartender.
"He'll be here in a few minutes," says the runner, "he just can't keep up with me."

Who is the fastest runner of all time?
Adam, because he was first in the human race!

What do you call a free treadmill?
Outdoors.

Lynne decided that she needed to do some altitude training – so she put her treadmill on top of the wardrobe.

I started as a Fun Runner doing 2k races on a Saturday but I soon caught the Running Bug. Quickly I progressed to being a Moderately Serious 10k Runner then a Fairly Sombre Marathon Runner and finally I graduated to become a Thoroughly Depressed Ultra Runner.

The Grand Old Duke of York said to his ten-thousand men, "Right you miserable lot – we're going to run to the top of the hill."
A little voice chirped from the crowd of soldiers, "Please Sir, can we make it an out-and-back?"

Colin was so obsessed with running he got a treadmill installed in his place of work – the passengers on his bus were furious.

Sharon and Douglas are running along a trail when they are suddenly confronted by a ginormous grizzly bear.
They freeze for a moment in terror but on hearing the bear's angry roar they both run like hell.
As they run Sharon unfastens her heavy backpack and throws it to the side of the track.
"That's not really going to help," said Douglas, "we will never be able to outrun a bear."
"Outrun the bear?" said Sharon, "I'm not trying to outrun the bear. All I need to do is outrun you!"

What do you call an ultra-runner with ten toenails?
A fraud.

Reflections on an Ultra-marathon . . .
During the Race:
This is shite - I'm in bloody agony.
Why the Hell am I doing this?
I'll never, ever run another ultra!!
+
Two Days after the Race:
That was amazing. I'm feeling ecstatic.
I so love long distance running.
When's my next ultra race?

It was the annual Wall Half-Marathon and Bricky MacMortar set off along with over 2000 other bricks to run the rather undulating course. All was going well when, 10 miles into the race, Bricky suddenly came to an abrupt halt.
"Keep going, keep running," shouted a friend in the crowd.
"I can't, I can't," sobbed Bricky sorrowfully, "I've hit the human."

Two gas service engineers, Frank and Ernest, are out checking meters in Easterhouse. Parking their van at the end of a long street they work their way along until they get to the other end. As they are taking the final reading, the old lady of the house watches with suspicion from her kitchen window.

Finishing the meter check, Frank challenges Ernest to a race back to the van.

They set off! But as they run down the street as fast as they can the old lady whizzes past them screaming "Help! . . . Help! . . . Help!"

Reaching the van the old lady stops for breath.

"What's wrong?" shouts Frank, "What's the panic?"

"When I saw you guys fiddling with my gas then running off," she gasps, "I figured I'd better run like Hell too!"

How do you know that you're an obsessive runner?
Your treadmill has done more miles than your car.

I was an alcoholic until I took up running. Running changed everything and now I'm completely tea-total.
Yeah, I found that, as a runner, I couldn't drink any more - the whisky refused to stay in the damn glass.

Coming out of a Sauchiehall Street pub after a long session of socialising, Gasher realised his current financial situation could adversely affect his long term economic plan. He thus decided to improve his fiscal circumstances with a bit of traditional Ned work - a little honest mugging.

He positioned himself at a nearby autobank and prepared to apply his artistry.

A few moments later a tall, lean man approached the autobank and withdrew £100. Immediately Gasher confronted him with a request for an interest free loan. The man looked Gasher up and down before punching him in the stomach and running away shouting, "You can't catch me mate, I'm a Park Runner."

A little later Gasher confronted another man and demanded a donation. This time the man stared at Gasher for a few seconds, gave him a Glasgow Kiss and ran away shouting, "You can't catch me mate, I'm a Park Runner."

Gasher decided that he needed to choose an easier target, so he stood patiently a little distance from the autobank. After thirty minutes a little, old lady approached the machine and withdrew £300.

"Are you a Park Runner?" asked Gasher grufly.

"No sonny, I'm not," replied the little old lady politely.

"So you've never, ever completed a Parkrun?" said Gasher menacingly.

"No, son, cross my heart and hope to die, I've never done a Parkrun," assured the little old lady.

Moving in close Gasher growled, "Give me all your money misses."

The little old lady slowly looked Gasher up and down. She looked at the money she was holding.

Then, without a word, the little old lady kicked Gasher hard between the legs and ran off.

Writhing on the ground in pain Gasher called after the little old lady, "You old bugger, you said you weren't a Park Runner!"

"That's right," replied the little old lady, "but my marathon time isn't bad."

I ran the Royal Parks Half-Marathon dressed as a peanut. Never again! Those squirrels are so scary!!

The Glenmore-24 is a twenty-four hour race held on a 4 mile loop near Inverness. Runners set off at midday and runs as far as they can in twenty-four hours.

At 2am, James, one of the top runner, spotted a slower runner, Ray, kneeling at the side of the track.

"Are you okay?," asked James.

"Yeah, yeah," replied Ray pensively, "just saying a wee prayer."

"Praying?" gasped James in surprise.

"Yeah, as I was running along I suddenly realised that this is my 200th ultra, so I thought I'd stop for a moment to chat to the Big Man."

"Oh right," laughed James, a little embarrassed, "so are you asking for a PB?"

"No," replied Ray slowly, "I'm asking him to let me break a leg so I can bloody well get my life back."

One rainy Saturday morning Noah is surprised to discover hundreds of the animals running round the deck.

"What on God's good Earth is going on," he enquired.

"We've organised an Ark Run," wheezed a pair of alligators as they ran by.

Sometimes Spot the Duck finds 95 mile races a little tiring.

Lisa was on the lookout for a new boyfriend when she spotted a good looking guy moving into the apartment next door. Over the next few days she noticed (without in any way being a stalker) that he went running every morning at precisely 5am. A plan was hatched. Lisa hurried down to the local sports shop and bought their very best, most expensive running gear. Next morning she went out while he was doing his warm-up routine.

"Going running?" she enquired.

"Yeah, doing 10 miles," replied Peter.

"Mind if I join you?" she asked.

He agreed and off they set at a steady pace. It took Lisa every ounce of energy to keep up with Peter but eventually they arrived back where they started. Wishing to appear fit and enthusiastic she asked if Peter wanted to do another ten miles. However to her disappointment Peter declined. Lisa slunk back to her apartment, pulled a sicky, and spent the day in bed recovering.

The next day Peter was doing speed work and Lisa joined him. They run up and down the street twenty times until they were both exhausted.

"That was great," lied Lisa. "Let's do it all over again only faster."

"No thanks," said Peter, "I need to get to work."

Lisa hobbled back to her apartment and spent the rest of the day watching television in bed in a desperate attempt to get some feeling back into her legs.

A few days later Lisa saw Peter heading out and once again she joined him. He said he was going for a gentle jog so, as Lisa ran alongside him they had the opportunity to chat. Eventually, Lisa plucked up the courage and asked him out on a date.

"Absolutely not - I couldn't possibly date you!" he said emphatically, "You are way too competitive for me."

Run every day – die healthy!

Karen and Elaine had been dating for four years when Karen decided it was time to pop the question. They were both keen runners so Karen wanted to make it extra special by proposing during the Paris marathon. They set off together but soon afterwards Karen ran off to find a romantic spot at which to propose. Eventually she found a beautiful spot where the route went along the River Seine. She knelt at the side of the road, ring at the ready, waiting for Elaine to come along.

Five minutes later Elaine came running along the river, spotted her girlfriend and stopped abruptly beside her.

"My dearest darling Elaine," said Karen, looking up at her exhausted, sweating girlfriend, "I love you with every breath I take, please marry me and make me the happiest woman in the world."

With that little speech she took the ring and held it out to her beloved.

"You ratbag!" Elaine replied throwing the ring into the huge crowd of runners who had stopped to watch, "You horrid, stinking ratbag! I was on for a great PB and you've bloody well gone and ruined it."

Halfway through a marathon: the Optimist thinks, "I'm already half way there", the Pessimist thinks "shit I've got another half to go" and the Realist thinks "for fuck sake my legs are bloody aching and I think I'm going to have a heart attack".

What I think about when I'm running . . .
. . . beer . . . chocolate . . . am I nearly there yet? . . . beer . . . chocolate . . . am I nearly there yet? . . .

Why are Marathon Runners like babies?
They all wear bibs, dribble their bottles and whine a lot.

Gavin entered the Dublin Marathon dressed as a penis. But sadly he pulled out after twenty miles because one of the marshals rubbed him up the wrong way.

Ross and Margarette met while running the Venice Marathon. They chatted away and got on so well that they almost forgot that they were in a race. They finished together and afterwards went for lunch. A whirlwind romance followed and the next year they married while running the Venice Marathon. They were so much in love with each other and with running that they wrote into their vows that 'as testimony to their love' they would complete the Venice Marathon together every single year.
They held true to that vow for ten years but in their eleventh year they rewrote them – 'as testimony to their love' they would complete the Venice Half-Marathon together every single year.
All went well for another eight years but as they aged and slowed they eventually rewrote their vows – 'as testimony to their love' they would complete the Venice 10k together every single year.
The 10k was enjoyable and they ran side by side each year giving each other a big hug as they crossed the finish line. But the years were not kind and they found the race getting harder and harder. They persevered for another seven years but on the eight Ross only just made it to the finish.
Can I make a suggestion?" he said to Margarette over lunch. "Let's change our vows again – let's make it that 'as testimony to our love' every single year we come to Venice and watch the Kiddies Fun Run!"

It was Christmas and Santa was delivering presents to all the good children around the world. As Rudolph pulled him in the sleigh over the North Sea, Santa was becoming increasing worried about the time, for they were taking much longer to deliver the presents than on previous years. Santa made the error of asking Rudolph if he was putting on weight and this sent Rudolph into such a huff that his nose very nearly stopped shining.

Rudolph felt gravely insulted! He was absolutely furious! He said that the reason they were going so slowly was that Santa was much fatter than he had ever been. A row developed and, as they flew across London, Santa suggested they settle who was the fattest by having a race. Angrily Rudolph dropped from the sky and landed the sleigh with a thud beside the Serpentine Lake in Hyde Park. "Twice round the lake," said Rudolph, "and the loser needs to go on a diet for the next three months."

So Santa and Rudolph set off running around the lake as fast as they could. In truth both Santa and Rudolph had put on a lot of weight since the previous Christmas and they struggled to get up any speed as they huffed and puffed along the path.

As this was going on, Marianne, and her five year old daughter, Julie, on their way home from a Christmas party, were walking through the park. From their vantage point above the lake, Marianne spotted Santa and Rudolph.

"Look honey," whispered Marianne, "look down by the lake."

"Oh mummy they look so funny," replied Julie with a giggle.

At this moment the two runners were approaching the finish and at the very last moment Santa overtook Rudolf. "I win! I win!" he shouted in glee.

"It's Santa and Rudolph," whispered Marianne.

"Mummy, mummy I don't believe it," said Julie sweetly, "I really, really don't believe it."

"You surely must believe in Santa now," said Marianne, "now that you've seen him and Rudolph for yourself." "Oh mummy dear I've always believed in Santa," whispered Julie softly, "I just don't believe that the big fat bastard can outrun a reindeer."

Recently I was asked whether I'd rather give up running or sex. No, dear wife, I am not falling for that one again.

Last year I entered my very first marathon. The race started and almost immediately I was in last place. It was embarrassing – I tried to keep up but my legs were like jelly. By mile 16 I was reduced to walking, trying my best to keep the slow runners in sight, but as I approached 26 miles I could only see one other runner and he was a hundred yards in front of me. Suddenly he stopped, 50 yards before the finish line. He turned round and watched me hobble painfully towards him.

"Hey ya loser," he jeered, "you're going to be last you big girl's blouse."

He did a silly Mo-Bot and laughing he shouted, "How does it feel to be last?"

"Do you really want to know?" I replied and, at that, I dropped out of the race.

Keith had had enough. His wife, Adeela, was spending all her time running, training and planning races. So Keith gave her an ultimatum, "You have until midnight on Saturday to decide – it's either running or me."

"It will have to wait until Sunday," said Adeela, dismissively, "I've got a really important marathon on Saturday."

Three athletes met by chance while waiting in the Departure Lounge at Heathrow Airport. Chat soon turned to sport.

"I just won a Major Tournament," said the tennis player, "earned myself £2 million. Not bad for playing seven games of tennis,"

"I just won a Major Tournament too," said the golfer, "earned myself a neat £1.4 million. Not bad for playing four games of golf."

"I'm on my way home after winning the Self-Transcendence 3,100 mile footrace," said the long distance runner, "took me forty-five days to complete - running about seventy miles each day."

"Bloody Hell!" said the other two in unison.

"What did you win for doing such a crazy thing?" asked the tennis player.

The long distance runner dug deep into his kit bag.

"Look at this beauty," he said proudly, carefully unwrapping his precious prize, "I won this fabulous little trophy."

Sometimes Spot the Duck can be a bit of a rebel.

Knock Knock,
Who's there?
. . . Who's there?
. . . . . . Who's there?
Mum, that jogger has knocked the door and run away
again!

Fiona, "I run every single morning."
Rosie, "Wow, I didn't know you were doing a runstreak!"
Fiona, "I'm not – I'm just always late for my train."

"I want you to take up running and run the Loch Ness
Marathon next year," said Old Doctor Langsyne.
"But doctor I'm eighty-three," gasped Dharam.
"Age is no barrier to running," said Old Doctor Langsyne
firmly.
"But I've got a dodgy knee. I can barely walk," complained
Dharam.
"This is for experimental research purposes," said Old
Doctor Langsyne reassuringly.
"Okay Doctor. I'll do it," said Dharam. "What is the
research?"
"Well I reckon that if I can get an old clapped-out-codger
like you to do it," said Old Doctor Langsyne, "then there's
hope that I could have a go myself some year."

Fifty Shades of Running :
Running or Sex? You decide!
* You often do it with random strangers.
* Doing it makes you all hot and sweaty.
* You take precautions when doing it – mainly by applying lots of Duct Tape and Blister Plasters.
* You enjoy going to the local park on a Saturday morning for a quickie.
* You have considered taking performance enhancing substances.
* You think about it six times every hour.
* Sometimes you start off too fast and need to pull out before the finish.
* You have fond memories of your best performances.
* You eat jelly babies while doing it.
* You have installed an electric machine in your cellar so you can sneak away to do it during spare moments.
* You once did it for 24 hours without stopping then couldn't walk for a week.
* You often do it on your own but it's not nearly as satisfying.
* Sometimes, when you're not doing it, you see others doing it and you feel jealous.
* You wear scanty, tight clothing when doing it.
* You boast about it to your mates.
* You keep a good supply of lubricant handy just in case.
* You have a collection of medals you got for doing it.
* Sometimes five times a week just isn't enough.
* As you get older you are able to keep going for longer – but you are so much slower.
* You worry that everyone else seems to be enjoying doing it more that you are.
* It annoys you when the person you're doing it with finishes before you.
* Sometimes the effort of doing it causes you an injury.
* You have a trainer to help you with technique.

* You once tried doing it on an aeroplane but there really wasn't enough room and it annoyed the other passengers.
* You hold cherished memories of the first time you did it.
* Sometimes when you do it you use a map and compass to guide you to the right zone.
* You love the applause you get as you finish doing it.
* You post hundreds of photos on Facebook of you doing it.
* After you have done it you often feel that you did not perform as well as you could have done.
* You once did it dressed as a chicken and raised £1000 for charity.
* You have a secret fantasy that one day you might do it professionally.
* A small trophy, sitting on your bookshelf, proudly testifies that, on one occasion, you were 3rd best in your age group at doing it.
* You have done it in the streets of Tokyo, Wellington, Manchester and Boston.
* You happily admit that, without your support team, there are times when you could not have done it.
* You have done it with a group of 50,000 others but much prefer more intimate sessions.
* Sometimes, before you start doing it, you like to wear a bin-bag.

FunRunFact: Knit One Purl One
The longest scarf knitted whilst running a marathon is 3.70 metres. It was knitted by American runner David Babcock at the Kansas City Marathon on the 19th October 2013.

Alice bought a running bra – but it was always too fast for her to keep up with.

Tips for Newbies:

* Be careful in your choice of trainers. If you buy the wrong type you will quickly destroy your knees. If you buy the right type you will slowly destroy your knees.

* Run for pleasure rather than to be highly competitive – though, admittedly, there is no greater pleasure in life than finishing ahead of a friend in a race.

* When training find your own comfortable running pace. If you black out after five minutes, you are probably running too fast. If workmen from the council come along and paint you yellow, you may be running too slowly.

* Do a warm-up before you set off on a training run. The best method is to down a large glass of Prosecco. If the urge to run still persists, double the amount of warm-up.

* Dogs can be a threat - especially in parks. If a huge, vicious dog charges after you and lunges at your throat, calmly say, "Down boy – good doggie". If that doesn't work, show him your membership card from the Dog Lovers Society.

* Never run in high-heeled shoes or wellington boots.

* Take care in your choice of nutrition for during races. Taking two or three energy gels during a marathon is probably okay. Taking a triple-decker hamburger with French Fries during a Parkrun is probably overkill.

* As you run along during training or at a race, people will shout encouraging remarks such as, "You're looking great," or "You're doing amazing". Don't be fooled into thinking that this in some way reflects on your ability as a runner. They are just having a laugh – secretly they are hoping that you will get far enough away from them before you have your heart-attack.

* Join a running club. Seeing you wearing your club vest at the start of a race will scare the shit out of the other newbies.

* If all else fails – walk. If walking fails – crawl. If crawling fails - feign an injury. That way you can DNF with a little bit of dignity still intact.

Running is even more addictive than eating prawn flavoured ice-cream while Morris Dancing. Once you've put on a pair of trainers you are hooked! Oh, at first, you may think that you'll never do anything harder than a Parkrun but before you know it you will be getting up in the middle of the night to search the internet for another 10k to enter. From there you will quickly progress to half-marathons and then marathons. After that the allure of the hard stuff cannot be resisted and monthly fixes of Ultra-Races will become your norm. Yes, when you've started there's no turning back . . . unless it's an out-and-back-race of course!

Running Club Rules:
* It's okay to be slow in races but it's not okay to be slow paying your club fees.
* Wear your club t-shirt with pride – and try to wash it occasionally.
* Never, ever outrun the club champion.
* During races help fellow club runners in distress – unless, of course, it would jeopardize a PB.
* You are a runner – an athlete. Do not, while wearing club colours, describe yourself as; a jogger, a back-marker, a plodder, a middle-of-the-packer or a fun-runner. Anyone found doing so will be immediately kicked out of the club.

Lorn and Barbara were on a training run.
"Let's make this more fun," said Lorn enthusiastically, "let's do some fartleks,"
"No, let's make it even better than that," replied Barbara, "let's go to the movies."

One evening Aazeen went to the prestigious Ealing Elite Athletics Association in the hope that she could become a member.
"Are you a serious runner," asked the Members Secretary in a rather derisory manner.
"Not really," relied Aazeen, "I like to tell the occasional joke or two."

Why didn't the dog want to take up running?
It was a boxer!

Dawn, "I've started training for my first marathon."
Scott, "That's fantastic – so what's the longest distance you've run?"
 "Oh I haven't run yet," replied Dawn, "I'm practicing the carbo-loading to see how that goes."

What did the pirate say on completing the Bahamas Marathon?
Too faaaarrrrghhhhh!

Pirate Mary-Rose completed the Rotorua Ekiden Marathon with her faithful parrot sitting on her shoulder.

As the race photographer snapper her crossing the finish line he yelped, "Wowzer – you must be exhausted doing a marathon with that old bird!"

"Nawww," squawked the parrot, "I'm feeling great."

Walt inadvertently strayed into the rough area of Manhattan. Before he realised his mistake he was surrounded by a group of knife carrying hooligans.

"Hand over your watch and iPhone," spat Mental Floss their leader.

"Oh give me a break," said Walt, trying not to show his fear, "I'm just an ordinary guy like you – how about at least giving me some sort of chance before you take my stuff."

"What would you suggest?" sneered Mental Floss, swiping his switchblade playfully in front of Walt.

"Give me a ten metres start and let that lad with skull and crossbones tattoo on his forehead chase me," stammered Walt, pointing at the smallest, weediest gang member he could spot. "If he can catch me I'll happily donate my watch, iPhone and my wallet to you."

Slowly and carefully, Mental Floss thought about Walt's proposal.

"Okay," he rasped, "let's do this."

"Wait a moment," said the weedy lad with skull and crossbones tattoo on his forehead, "this is dumb – I could never catch him - I haven't run since I was a kid."

"Calm it," demanded Mental Floss, "to even things up we're going to race at the gym and our smart-arsed friend here will be running on a treadmill!"

Goodie Bags - What you don't want to get:
A pre-used pair of running socks.
An XXXXXXXX-large size technical t-shirt.
A 10% discount voucher for a charity shop.
10 massive bags of potatoes.
A voucher for a blind-date with the grumpy old marshal
you insulted at Check-Point 3.
A year's supply of Marmite
Free entry to their next race!

If you think a minute passes really quickly try spending it on a treadmill.

You burn around 2,688 calories during a marathon.
Just think – that lets you eat 272 M&Ms or drink 33 glasses
of Prosecco!
Now that makes it all worthwhile!!!

Funniest Relay Team Names:
* Puns on the run.
* Are we almost there yet?
* To lazy to run the whole way.
* We couldn't thing of a funny name.
* Our shorts are longer than our training runs.
* We can't be bothered.
* Too slow to care.
* Spongebob Slowpants.
* Would rather take a Uber.
* Run long and perspire.
* Abominable Slowmen.
* Sisters with blisters.
* Not fast – just furious.
* Old gits running.
* Mission Impossible.
* Blood, Sweat and Beers.
* Girls just wanna have run.
* How the West was run.
* Alice in Runderland.
* All for run and run for all.
* Four groan men.
* 50 shades of awesome.
* Run like the winded.
* Agony on De Feet.
* It is better to have run and lost than never run at all.
* Victorious Secret.
* Your pace or mine.
* If we had 4 faster runners we could be a winning team.
* Mind over miles.
* Losers and boozers.
* You're never too slow to be a runner.
* Dashing Divas.
* We thought they said rum!
* Relay on us.
* Slow runner – please don't pass.

* Don't blame me.
* After six cocktails this seemed like a good idea.
* Men on a Mission.
* We lost the bet!
* Who's stupid idea was this?
* Please enter team name here.

Why did Josephine run for four hours but only move 2 feet?
Because she only has two feet.

There is no race too long or too short that the thought of a cold refreshing beer can't help spur you on to a sprint finish on the final 500 metres . . . well perhaps with the exception of a 100 metre race.

Clark did so much cross-training his wife made him go on an anger-management course.

The collective noun for sheep is a flock.
The collective noun for fish is a school.
What is the collective noun for runners?
A race!

Pain Now

Vodka Later

What's the first thing a runner does on receiving an invitation to his sister's wedding?
Check his race diary to see if he is able to go.

"I've just completed my first half-marathon," said Robin.
"Well done," exclaimed Anne. "Did you do the first half or the second half?"
"No you daftie," said Robin sarcastically, "I did the middle half."

"Today is a very important day in my running career," said Gillian to her husband, "Today marks the 500th day in my Runstreak of Rest Days."

.

**Mary had a little lamb,
She raced it round the zoo,
The lamb ran way too fast,
So she made it into stew.**

FunRunFact: Record Breakers
The IAAF world record for men is 2:02:57, set by Dennis Kimetto of Kenya on September 28, 2014 at the Berlin Marathon. The IAAF recognizes two world records for women, a "Mixed Gender" record of 2:15:25, set by Paula Radcliffe of the United Kingdom on April 13, 2003 at the London Marathon, and a "Women Only" record of 2:17:01, set by Mary Keitany, on April 23, 2017 at the London Marathon.

**When not running ultras
Spot the Duck
trains to be an
astronaut.**

Rob takes up running but, as he's slow and nervous about it all, he doesn't tell his friends. After some late night training in the dark he plucks up courage to enter a 10k race. All goes well so the next month he completes a half-marathon. Delighted at his achievement he goes home, gets changed, and heads to his local pub for a celebratory drink. However, when he gets there, he finds that none of his friends want to talk to him – in fact they totally shun him. Rob is bewildered and, near to tears, heads out of the pub. As he reaches the door his best friend pulls him aside and explains why nobody is talking to him.

Shocked by what he hears, Rob hurries home to confront his mother.

"Mum, if you need to brag to everyone about what I've been doing," he yells angrily, "tell them that I run races – don't go saying to everyone in the town that I am a racist."

"Do you mind if a take a shortcut across your field," Neil asked the farmer, "I'm in a cross-country race and if I shave a few minutes I might come third."

"No problem," replied the farmer, "and if you meet my bull you might even come in first."

Sign that you're an experienced distance runner: You are sitting in a traffic jam thirty miles from your destination and you ask yourself, "Why the heck did I decide to drive rather than run?"

What do you call a runner with a stress fracture?
Anything you want – he won't be able to catch you!

In March Noanie prays to God: "Dear Lord, please let me win the D33 Ultra."

In April Noanie begs the Lord again: "Please make it so that I win the Highland Fling Ultra."

In June Noanie again prays: Please, please, dear Lord, let me win the Glen Lyon Ultra."

In July Noanie is sitting in church moaning to the Lord that he didn't help her win any of the races.

Suddenly she hears the roar of thunder and an almighty voice booms from the Most High: "For Christ sake Noanie, meet me half-way will you please – try running in one of the races instead of just marshalling."

"I've got myself a personal trainer," Giocomo told his running friend.

"Crikey! You must be keen – those guys are not cheap," replied Debbie.

"Too right," said Giocomo, "it's cost me $2,000 over the last 10 months."

"And are you running any faster now?" asked Debbie.

"Well not really," confessed Giocomo.

"And the New York Marathon," quizzed Debbie, "Did you achieve the PB time you were desperate to get?"

"No, I had a bit of a bad run," replied Giocomo pensively.

"So why the Hell are you paying for a person trainer?" interrogated Debbie.

"Well before, if I didn't do well, I'd beat myself up. For days I would feel really annoyed with myself," said Giocomo. "Now that I've got a trainer I can just blame him – that's well worth $200 a month!"

Kevin and Kirsty were busy playing in the bedroom when Kirsty heard the sound of footsteps coming along her hallway.

"Oh my God," she whispered, a little too loudly in her panic, "that's my husband. He'll murder you. You'd better get out quickly."

Scooping up his clothes from the floor, Kevin threw open the bedroom window and jumped the ten metres to the street below. It was a miserable, wet night but Kevin wasn't going to waste time putting on his clothes for he knew Kirsty's husband was an extremely jealous man and that he carried a gun. Kevin ran as fast as he could. As it happened the local running group were going by and caught up with Kevin.

"Do you always run in the nude?" asked Iona the group coach.

"Oh yeah," replied a very embarrassed Kevin, "I love feeling the air blow over my body as I run."

"And do you always run carrying your clothes over your arm?" quizzed Iona.

"Well yeah," replied Kevin, trying to come up with a convincing lie, "I run to Penn Station, pull on my clothes and get the train back home."

"Right," said Iona, rather unconvinced, "And do you always wear a condom when you're running?"

"No of course not," snapped Kevin, "only when it's raining!"

You know you're an ultra-runner when you are being introduced to new people and you categorise them; possible running buddy, possible support crew, possible pacer, possible hook-up for some post-race casual sex . . .

Great reasons not to jog:
* Christian Louboutin do not do running shoes.
* Fun Run? My idea of fun is sipping a Margarita on a warm Caribbean beach.
* I have an allergy to seeing people in ultra-tight lycra.
* I don't want to put Uber drivers out of work.
* I'm on a 45 year non-runstreak that I don't want to break.
* Would that mean having to get up from my sofa?
* I couldn't find a suitable pair of trainers for someone who procrastinates.
* Sweat is way too unfashionable.
* I once tried a 5k Parkrun – that was the worst 4 hours of my life.
* I get all the exercise I need walking to the donut shop.
* My best friend has a sore knee.
* I don't want to get my expensive trainers dirty.
* Running generates heat and that causes Global Warming.
* It might interfere with my main hobbies – watching television and drinking beer.
* I look so sexy in shorts it wouldn't be fair on the other runners.
* Why run? There has never been a point precisely 26.219 miles away that I've needed to get to urgently!
* Deep in my heart I have a passion for running – but the news hasn't reached my legs yet.
* It's too hot / cold / wet / dry / long / short / pink / boring / difficult / easy / impossible (delete as appropriate).
* I suffer from tachophobia.

You know you're a real ultra-runner when no one believes you when you say, "never again".

Mark the Millipede and Ada the Ladybird met up at the start of the Keukenhof Gardens Race.
"Good luck," shouted Ada to her friend, as she set off with the faster runners.
"Yeah," replied Mark, "have a good one."
Twenty-Five minutes later Ada finished, delighted to have got a PB. She was surprised to spot Mark for she knew that he was not the best of runners.
"You must have shifted," she said, "I can't believe that you finished before me!"
"Finished?" replied Mark, "Oh, I'm not finished – I'm still putting on all my running shoes."

Men 6521 BC: I just invented the wheel.
Men 1296: I just invaded Scotland.
Men 1492: I just discover America.
Men 1845: I just caught and killed a buffalo.
Men 1953: I just built my own house.
Men 2017: I just completed a Parkrun.

I can't believe I forgot to do my jog today – that's seven years in a row.

To relieve the boredom of fishbowl life, Chips the Goldfish and Cheese the Goldfish agreed to have a race. Chips was faster than Cheese and after about 20 minutes he caught up with his friend.
"I've done 50 laps around the bowl," said Chips cheerfully, "how about you?"
"Laps?" replied Cheese, "I thought we were doing an out-and-back!"

Clark approaches the club coach and asks, "Can you teach me how to do squats?"
"Sure," replies the coach, "how flexible are you?"
"Well," says Clark, "I can do Mondays and Thursdays."

When Alison started running she was delighted about how good she felt but was very embarrassed that she had bad flatulence every time she ran. So she went to see her doctor and asked if he could give her something for wind. So he gave her a kite.

I wouldn't say our new club member was slow, but last night he ran a bath and came second.

"I took up long distance running in an effort to stop worrying," confided Craig.
"Did it work?" asked his friend, Alexa.
"Not really," replied Craig, "now I worry about whether I'll be able to find my way home."

Everyone's
a
winner -
just don't
let me
be
LAST.

I've decided to run a marathon for charity. I didn't want to do it at first, but apparently it's for blind and disabled kids so I recon I've got a good chance of winning.

Eighty miles into the Lost Soul Ultra, Heather spots David at the checkpoint wearing his distinctive yellow marshal's jacket.

"You marshalling again, you nutter," she gasps as she unpacks the contents of her drop-bag, "you really must love the atmosphere and camaraderie of long distance races."

"Not really," grinned David, "I just love seeing people in total agony."

Why do marathon runners eat bananas?
Because gorillas are too smart to run marathons.

A group of runners turned up at the Cardiff 10k each dressed as a different font.

"You guys are barred," said the race director, "I don't want your type in my race."

Wee Willie Winkie runs through the town,
Upstairs and downstairs in his nightgown,
"Right you," yelled the Race Director, "you're disqualified for not carrying a foil blanket and waterproof jacket."

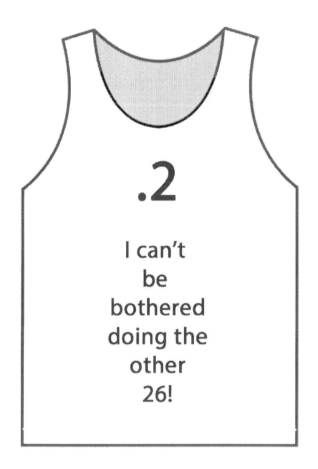

.2

I can't
be
bothered
doing the
other
26!

Greg fell off a ladder and was rushed to the local hospital. After having numerous x-rays done, the consultant explained to Greg that he his left leg was broken and he had multiple fractures of his right arm.

"Be straight with me doctor," said Greg earnestly, "does that mean I should or shouldn't run the marathon at the weekend?"

About the Author

Stuart was born at a very young age. From the start he showed no aptitude for running, in fact for the first year of his life he could barely be bothered to walk.

His loathing for running and all physical exercise was further cultivated during his long detention in the institution his parents referred to as 'school'.

During those long, hard school years many attempts were made to torture Stuart into doing extreme physical tasks such as jumping over wooden boxes, climbing ropes, hitting round objects with pieces of wood and running after balls in rectangular shaped 'pitches'. But, even then, Stuart was made of stern stuff and, as often as possible, escaped these sadistic punishments by locking himself in the toilets or escaping from the institution to find temporary sanctuary at the Fish and Chip Shop.

(Photograph at Loch Katrine Marathon taken by Fiona Rennie)

The next thirty or so years are a blur – mainly because I can't be arsed writing about them and you, dear reader, can't be arsed reading about them.

At the age of 51, having lived a fairly happy, sedentary life, and thoroughly looking forward to that slow decline into senile dementia and rheumatism, Stuart was suddenly forced out of his cosy armchair and onto the cruel roads in little more than his underwear. "You need to get some exercise!" exclaimed his son, Brian, and daughter, Amanda, "start running!"
Well he did 'run' with them around the block – a distance of 1km and, apart from having to walk 999 meters of the way, it was fairly successful.
But the agony was not allowed to stop there – oh no – he was ejected from his armchair and made to hobble, limp crawl and occasionally run around the block on a regular basis.

"Why not enter a 10k race?" one of his tormentors said, rather forcefully one day. And so, grudgingly and with a few moans, he undertook the 'M77 – Run the Road' race in spring 2005. Much to the surprise of everyone who knew him he managed to run the whole 10,000 metres and didn't die at the finish line. And so more, many more 10k races followed.

Running must have been having a strange effect on his brain for he suddenly had an urge to run a half-marathon – so, on a miserable autumn day (with rain, sleet and gale force winds) in 2005 he found himself at the starting line of the Jedburgh Half-Marathon. Having survived this he vowed that he'd never do another – ever, ever again. But by the time he'd driven home from Jedburgh he was desperate to have another go and immediately went onto the Scottish Athletics website and signed up for the next available race.

Of course he'd never attempt anything more than a 'half' . . . until Amanda bought him "The London Marathon: The History of the Greatest Race on Earth" – the experience sounded so amazing - he was hooked – he had to have a go.

By this time he'd joined "Bellahouston Road Runners" and was lucky enough to get a club place in the 2007 Marathon. Running 26.2 miles through the streets of London in 27 degree heat was an experience in more ways than one – but he got to the finish line in one piece.

. . . but London would definitely be his first and last marathon . . . well not quite – he had reached that level of insanity when he wanted more – so he completed the Edinburgh Marathon a month after London and the Loch Ness Marathon later that year.

Not satisfied with marathon distance Stuart soon began to look for longer races. His first ultra was the 35 mile Draycote Ultra – doing loops around the Draycote Water reservoir.

Stuart has now completed 31 marathons and 52 ultra-marathons. Half way through each of these races he has made a vow to himself that 'this is definitely the last'.

Some running facts about Stuart:

Runstreak:
Stuart has been doing a runstreak for more than six years –
here are a few statistics:
Number of Days of Runstreak: 2250
Minimum Daily Distance: 5km (3 miles)
Average Daily Distance: 12.67km (7.87 miles)
Total Distance Covered: 28,535 km (17,730 miles)

Running Tour de Scotland:
During 2015 Stuart completed a running adventure which
consisted of 3 parts:

Part 1: January : John Muir Way – 135 miles from Helensburgh to Dunbar
Stuart completed this coast to coast route from Helensburgh
on the West of Scotland to Dunbar on the East, over 3 days.
Unfortunately he took a stress fracture of the shin on the
first day and ran over 100 miles in considerable pain (not
the smartest thing to do – don't try this at home).

Part 2: August : Kielder (on the Scottish Border) to Muckle Flugga (on Shetland – the most northerly part of Britain) : 587 miles in 28 days
Stuart completed this run using a mixture of hill-running,
trails (West Highland Way and Great Glen Way) and roads.
(He can testify that running the A9 & A99 from Inverness
to Wick is something to be avoided).

Part 3: November : Villages: 26 villages A to Z – average marathon per day

Over 26 days, Stuart ran from his home to 26 different villages. To make it more fun he did them in alphabetical order; Aberfoyle, Balloch, Coatbridge etc.

X and Z proved a bit of a problem. As a solution he used IbroX for X – choosing a route that would create the letter X. For Z the best he could come up with was LenZie.

Scottish Ultra Marathon Series Championship – Over 60s Category

Stuart came 3rd in 2013 and 1st in 2016

Races Completed (April 2005 to August 2017)

Parkruns: 15
10ks: 48
Other Distances: 20
Half-Marathons: 19
Marathons: 31
Ultra Marathons: 52

Longest Ultras Stuart has completed:

West Highland Way Race (95 miles) – 3 times
Glenmore 24 hour race (Best distance 107 miles) – 4 times
Great Glen Race (72 miles)

Email: stuart@stuartmacfarlane.com

Stuart's other books include:

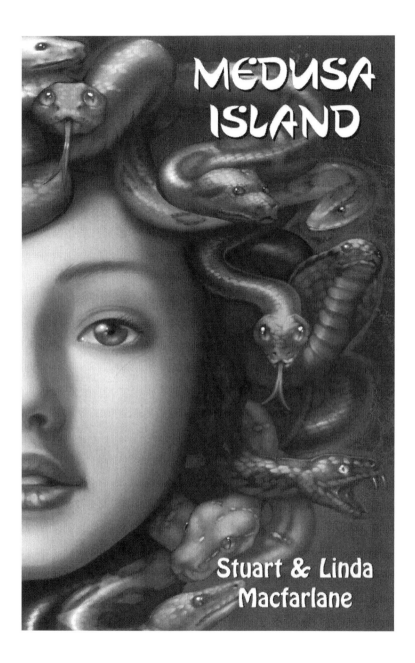

MEDUSA
ISLAND

Stuart & Linda
Macfarlane

Medusa Island

Evil scientist, Doctor X, has found a way to turn people and animals into mythical creatures. Already he's transformed everyone on the little Scottish Island of Gogha – now he plans to take over the whole world. Eleven year old Melissa has been changed into Medusa, with wriggling snakes in her hair. She escapes to the mainland to seek help but quickly discovers that anyone who looks at her turns to stone. Then Simon and Ross turn up - their sunglasses protect them from Melissa's powers. Only the three children can save the world. Somehow they must get to Doctor X and put a stop to his evil scheme. But with the island overrun by Harpies, Minotaurs, Chimeras, a Nine-Headed-Hydra and a host of other vicious creatures this will be a very dangerous task.

Extract: They kept running; running for their lives. Ahead of them a second Minotaur leapt out from behind a parked truck. They crashed to a halt. They were trapped. In a matter of seconds their flesh would be ripped from their bones in a frenzied bloodbath.

"Stare at it," commanded Simon. "Stare at it and turn it to stone."

"I am staring," cried Melissa. "Nothing's happening."

"Well stare harder," bellowed Simon. "Come on Melissa." Melissa stared straight into the huge beast's angry eyes willing it to turn to stone. With an eternity of hate the beast glared back. The rancid heat from his breath engulfed Melissa, burning her lungs with fear. The Minotaur's roar spat across her face. He obviously was not stone.

Stuart & Linda Macfarlane

The Secret
Diary of
Adrian Cat

The Secret Diary of Adrian Cat

Adrian is no ordinary cat – he has ambitions. Not only does he want to become the most famous cat in the world but he's also determined to create world peace between cats, dogs and mice.

Adrian's life is full of complications! In an attempt to win the affections of the power crazed, but beautiful, Snowball he is forced to join a gang run by the most evil cat in town - Killer. But Killer also loves Snowball and he's not going to let Adrian steal her away – not without a fight. On top of all of this Adrian has many adventures; he goes treasure hunting with a pirate parrot, saves the life of a fox and helps his best friend out of all sorts of trouble.

Whether you are nine or ninety-nine you will delight in Adrian's escapades and mishaps so join him in his thrilling adventures and discover whether he can overcome all his problems to find love, fame and happiness.

"The Secret Diary of Adrian Cat" is a hilarious account of one-year in the life of Adrian Cat - perfect for teenagers and adults. It contains some very funny sophisticated humour.

<<< EXTRACT >>>>

Sunday March 2nd
Today I had an intellectual day - Snowball would be impressed (if we were speaking).

Wrote a poem entitled DesideCata. I am thinking of becoming a cat laureate!

DesideCata

Stroll placidly amid the noise and haste and remember what peace there may be in a long tranquil nap. As far as possible, without being in any way humble, be on good terms with all creatures - with the obvious exception of dogs. Meow your desires loudly and clearly and occasionally listen to others, even your human, for she may be calling you for dinner. Avoid the company of fleas, they are vexations to both spirit and body. Enjoy your achievements - particularly wallpaper lovingly scratched and pieces of string thoroughly chased. Keep interest in your career, there will always be a need for good mousers in the changing fortunes of time. Be yourself; especially do not feign affection - except when you need a warm lap to sleep on. Neither be cynical about the love of cream, for through your charmed and enchanted existence it is as perennial as the grass it comes from.

Take kindly the council of the years and rejoice in the fact that you have nine lives.

Nurture arrogance of spirit to shield you from sudden misfortune such as getting stuck up a tree. But do not distress yourself with imaginings. Many fears are born out of getting less than twenty hours sleep in a day. Beyond a wholesome discipline be gentle with yourself and groom yourself frequently. You are a cat of the universe, so much greater than humans and dogs; you have a right to be served. And even though you may sleep through most of it, no doubt the universe is unfolding as it should. With all its snacks, adventures and peaceful dreams, it is truly a beautiful world. Be content. Continue to be happy.

www.thesecretdiaryofadriancat.com

A few of Stuart's books published by Exley Publications:

Printed in Great Britain
by Amazon